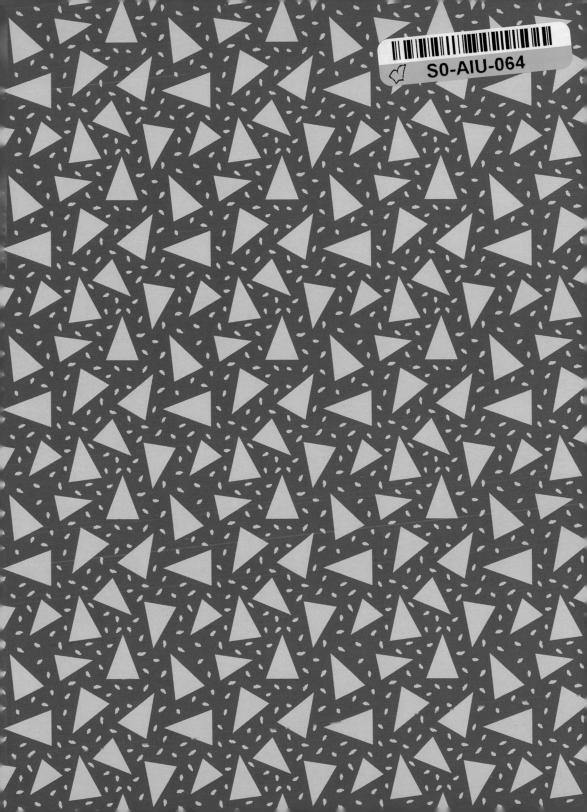

To Gareth:
the Rat to my Gnome

GNOME and Rat

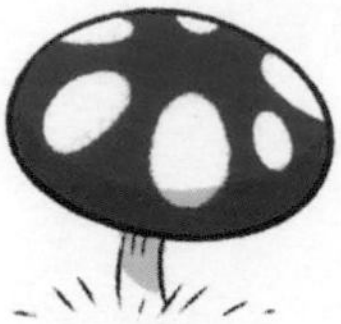

THIS IS A BORZOI BOOK PUBLISHED BY ALFRED A. KNOPF

Visit us on the Web! rhcbooks.com

Educators and librarians, for a variety of teaching tools, visit us at RHTeachersLibrarians.com

Library of Congress Cataloging-in-Publication Data is available upon request.

ISBN 978-0-593-48782-2 (trade) — ISBN 978-0-593-48783-9 (lib. bdg.) —
ISBN 978-0-593-48784-6 (ebook)

The text of this book is set in 22-point Gnome and Rat.

The illustrations in this book were created with tiny invisible paintbrushes and bottomless buckets of digital paint.

Interior design by Sarah Hokanson

MANUFACTURED IN CHINA

10 9 8 7 6 5 4 3 2 1

First Edition

GNOME and Rat

Lauren Stohler

Alfred A. Knopf 🐎 New York

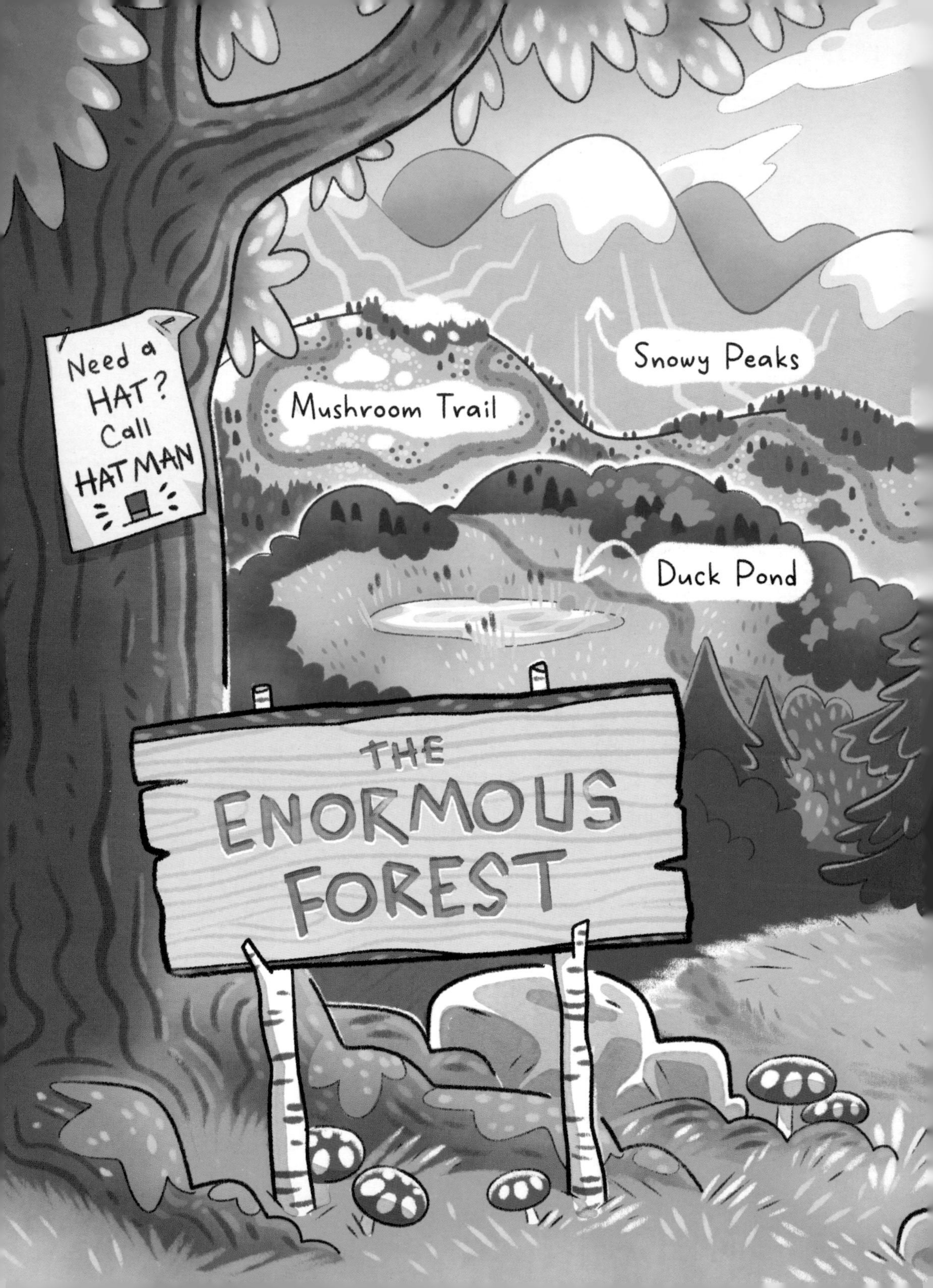
Need a HAT? Call HATMAN
Snowy Peaks
Mushroom Trail
Duck Pond
THE ENORMOUS FOREST

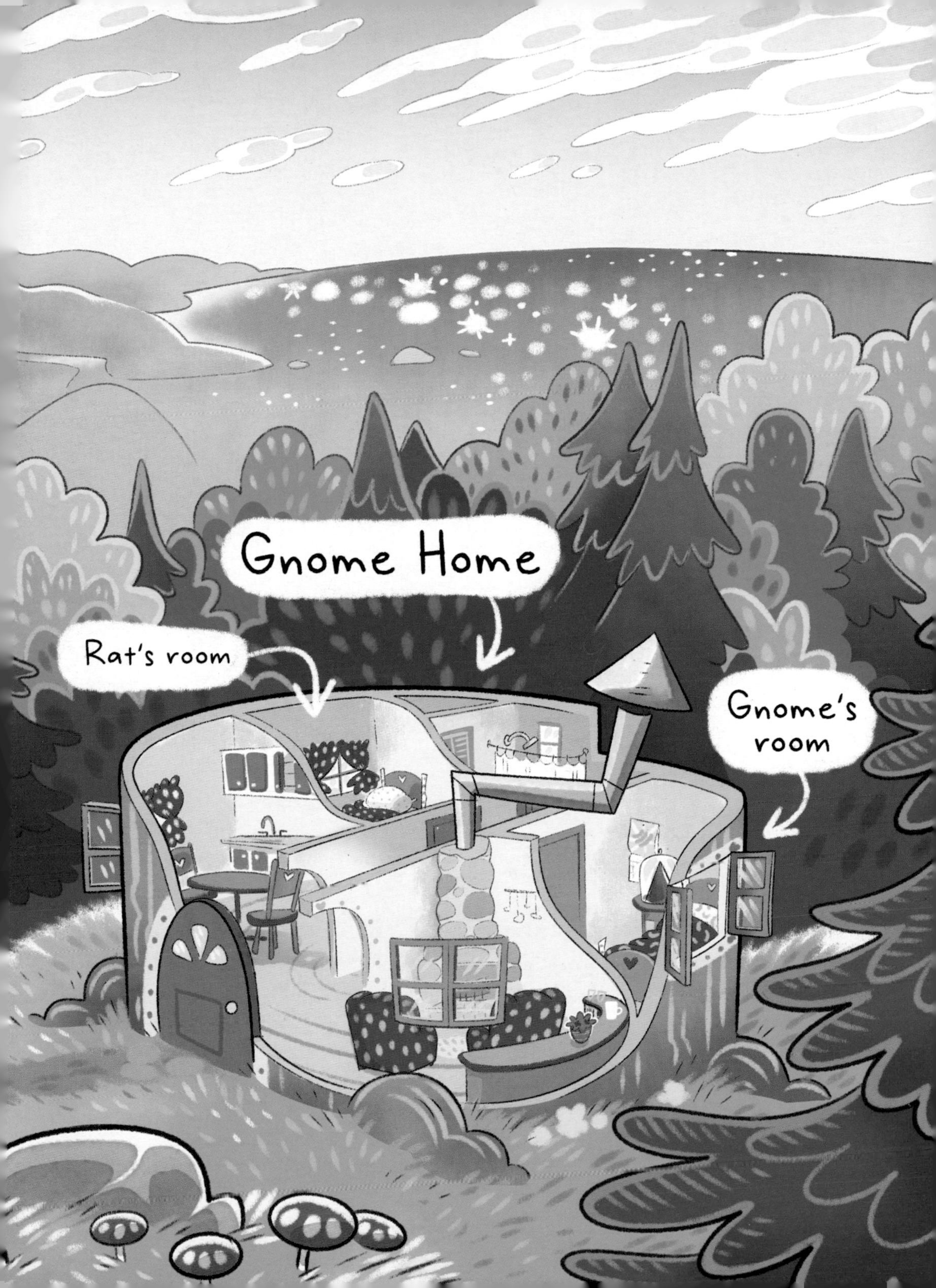
Gnome Home
Rat's room
Gnome's room

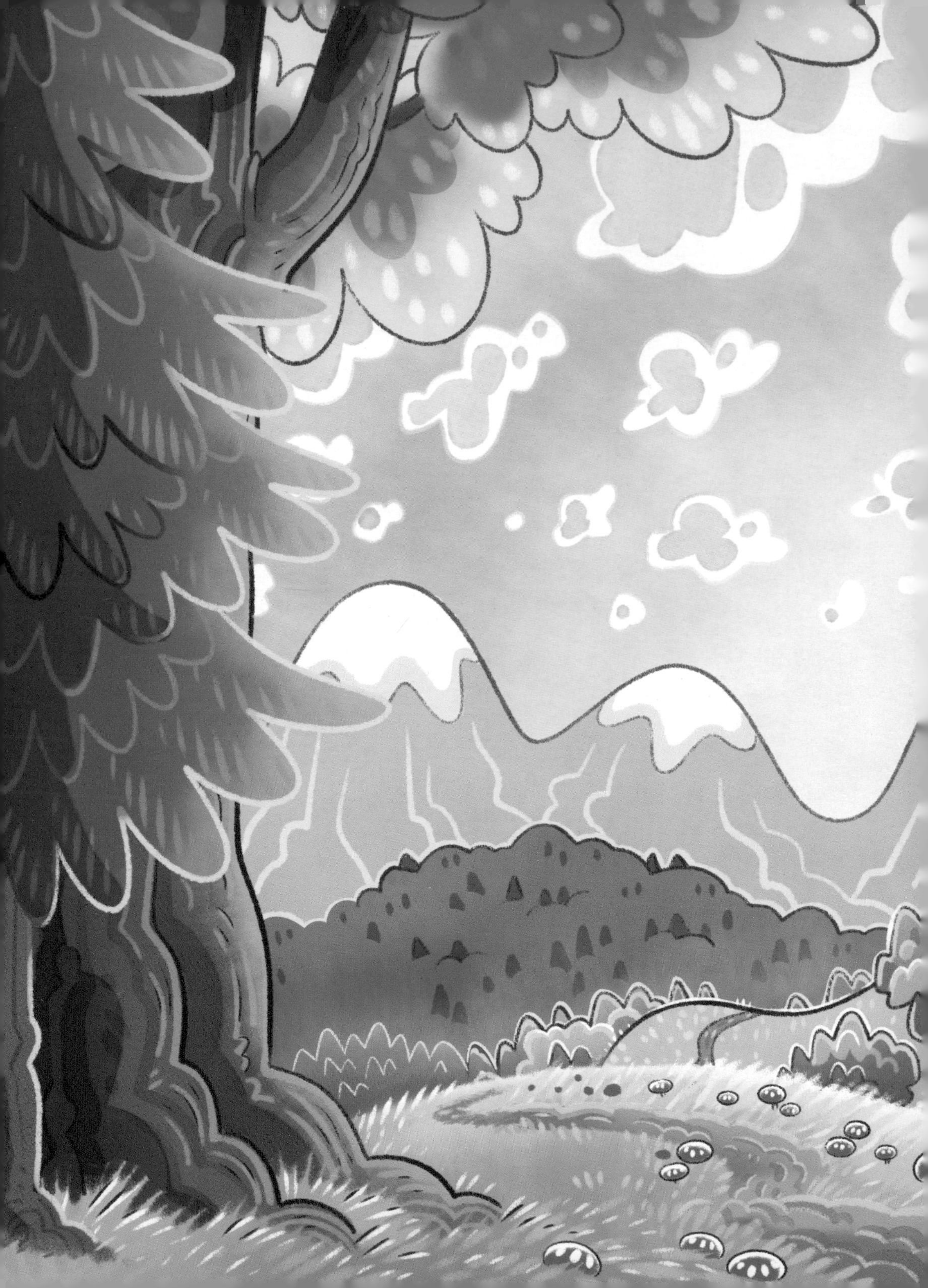

Contents

CHAPTER 1

Hat Day

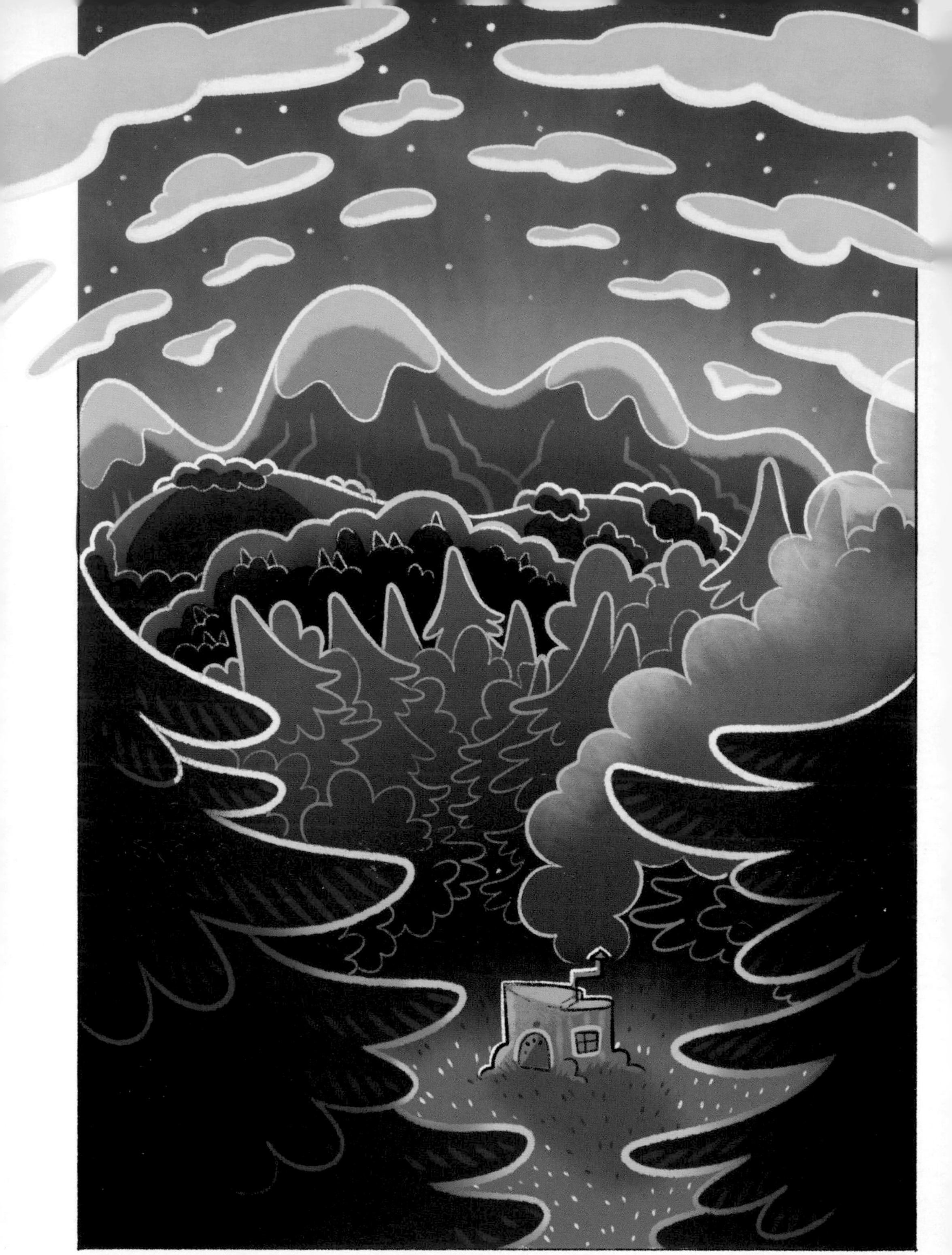

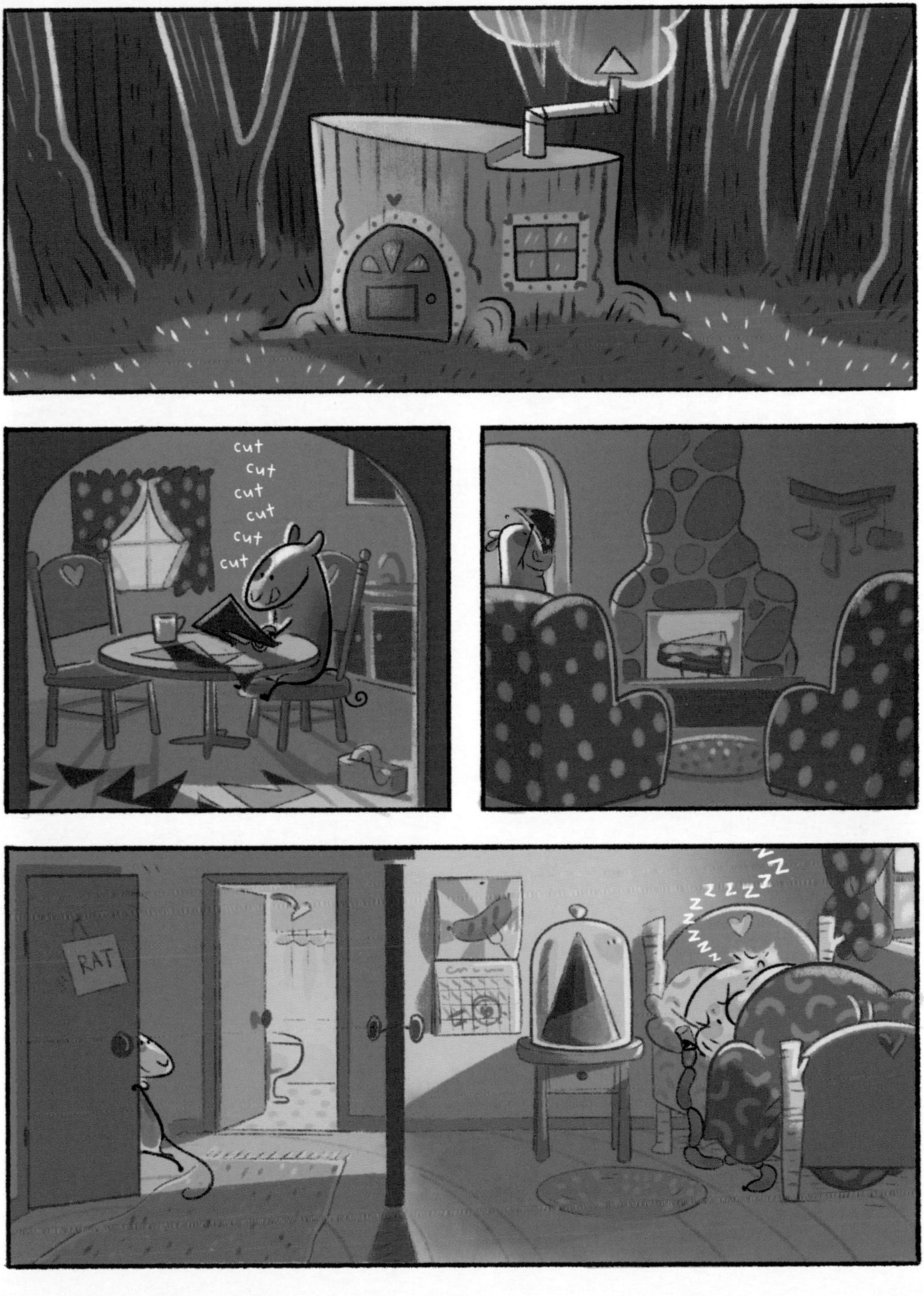
cut
cut
cut
cut
cut
cut
RAT

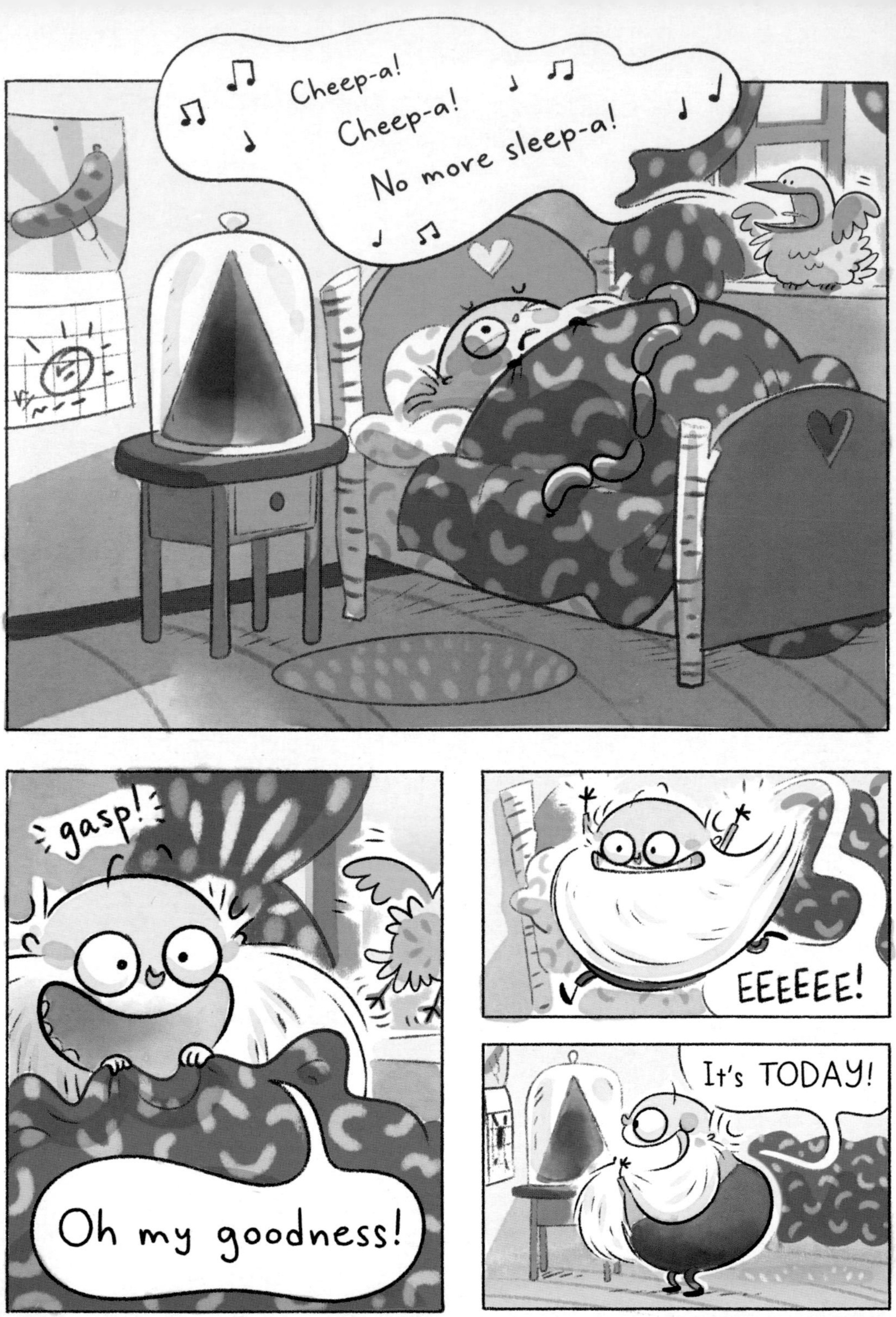
Cheep-a!
Cheep-a!
No more sleep-a!
gasp!
Oh my goodness!
EEEEEE!
It's TODAY!

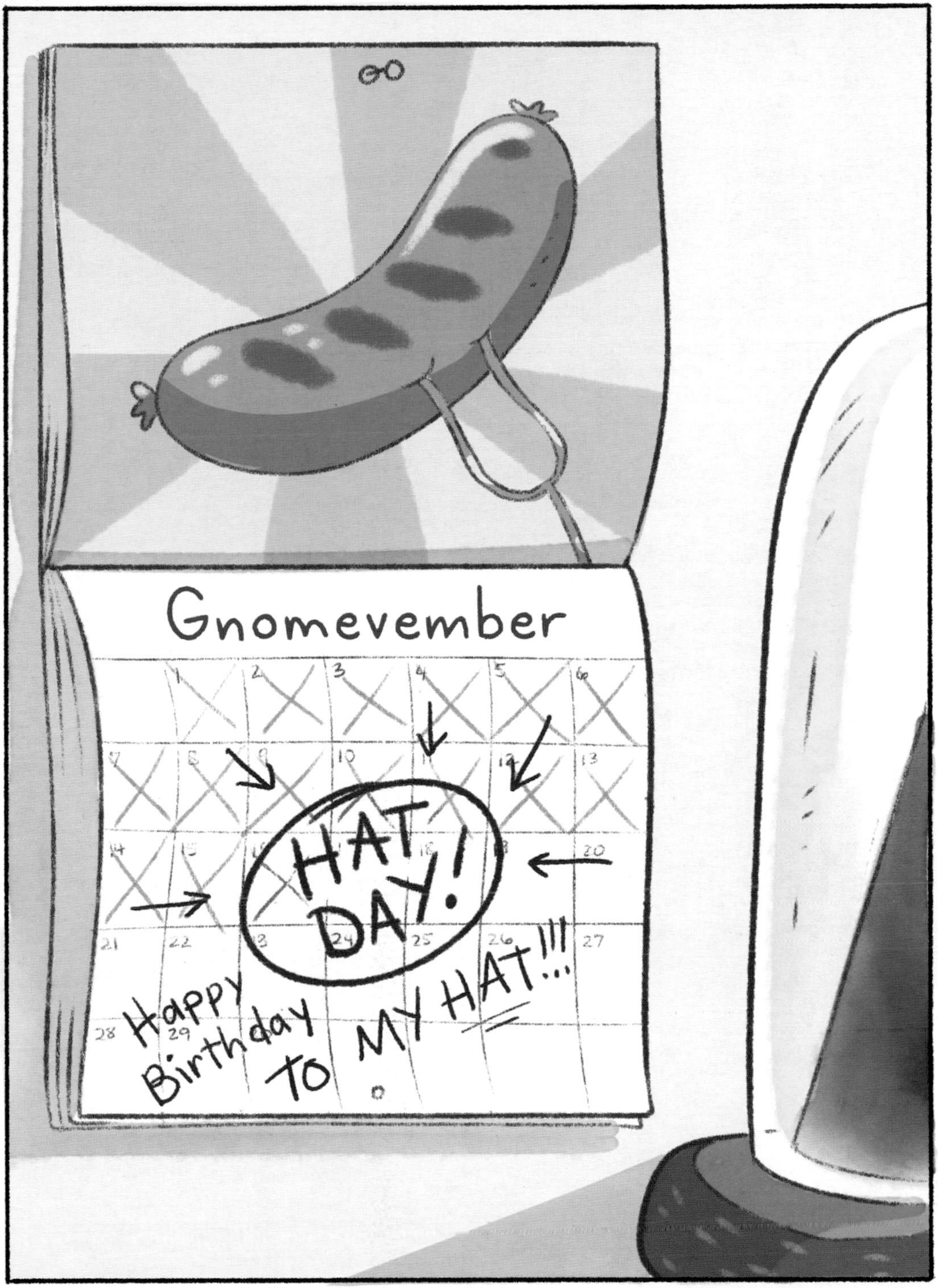
Gnomevember
HAT DAY!
Happy Birthday TO MY HAT!!!

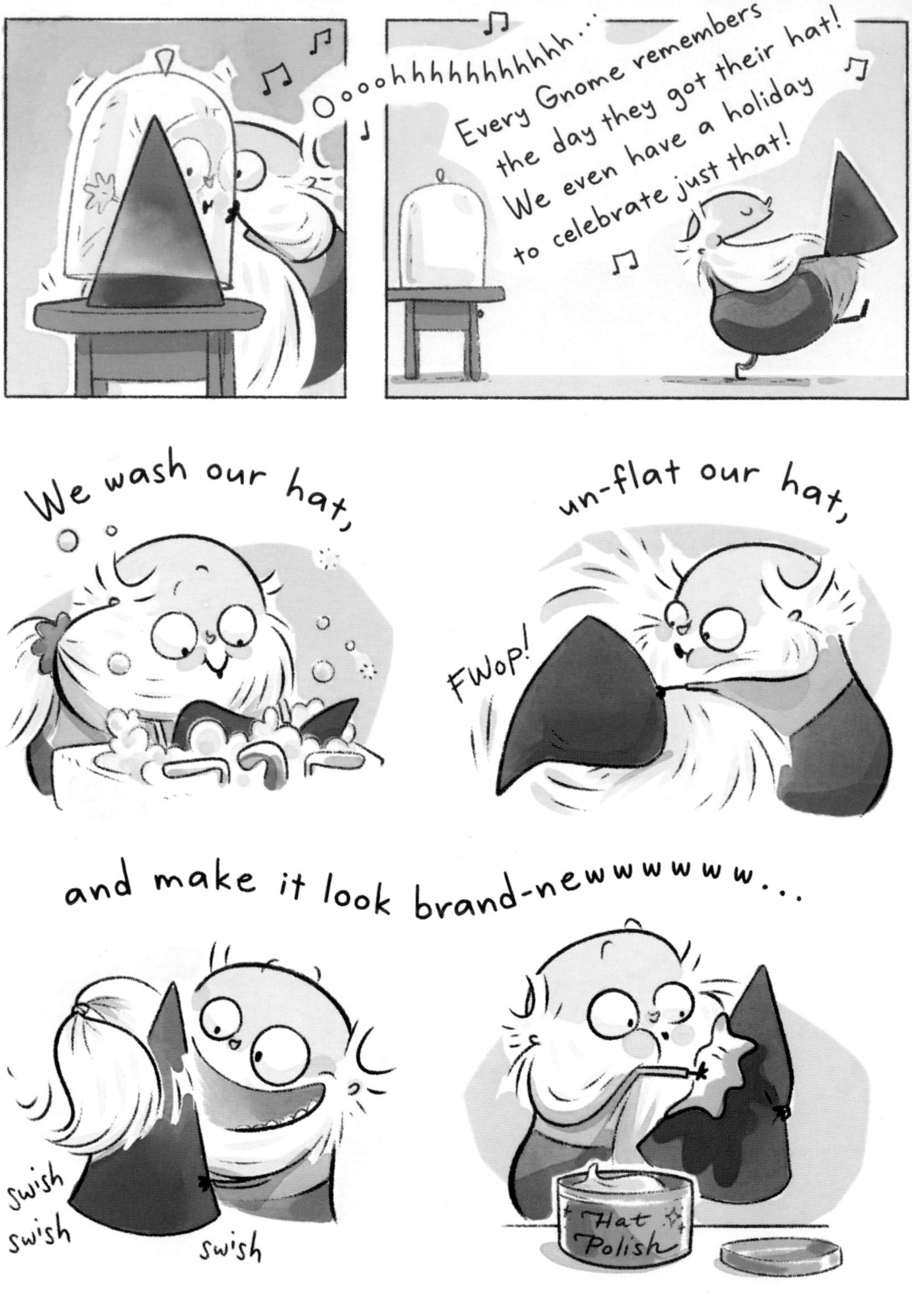
Oooohhhhhhhhhhh...
Every Gnome remembers the day they got their hat!
We even have a holiday to celebrate just that!
We wash our hat,
un-flat our hat,
FWOP!
and make it look brand-newwwwww...
swish
swish
swish
Hat Polish

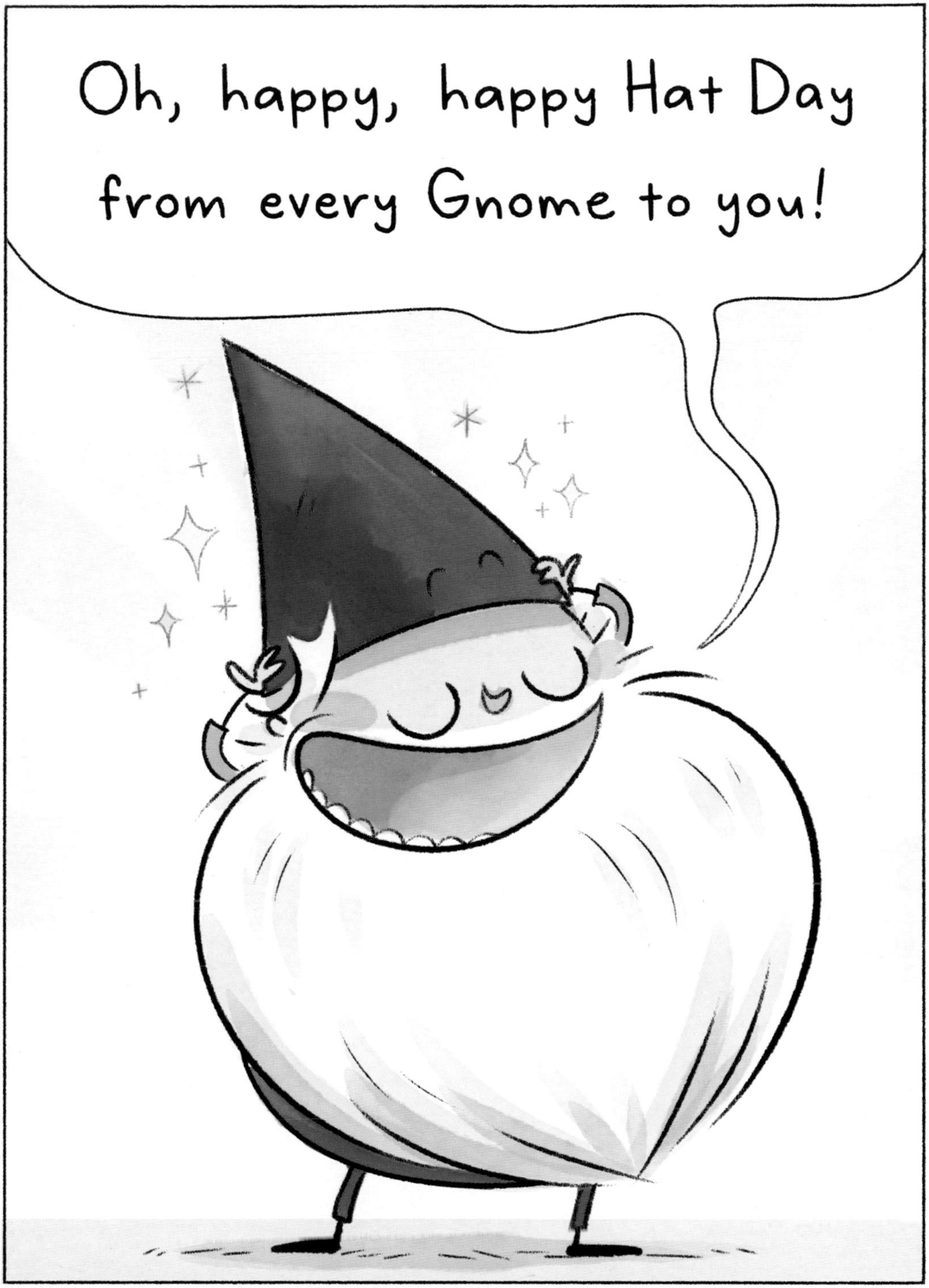
Oh, happy, happy Hat Day from every Gnome to you!

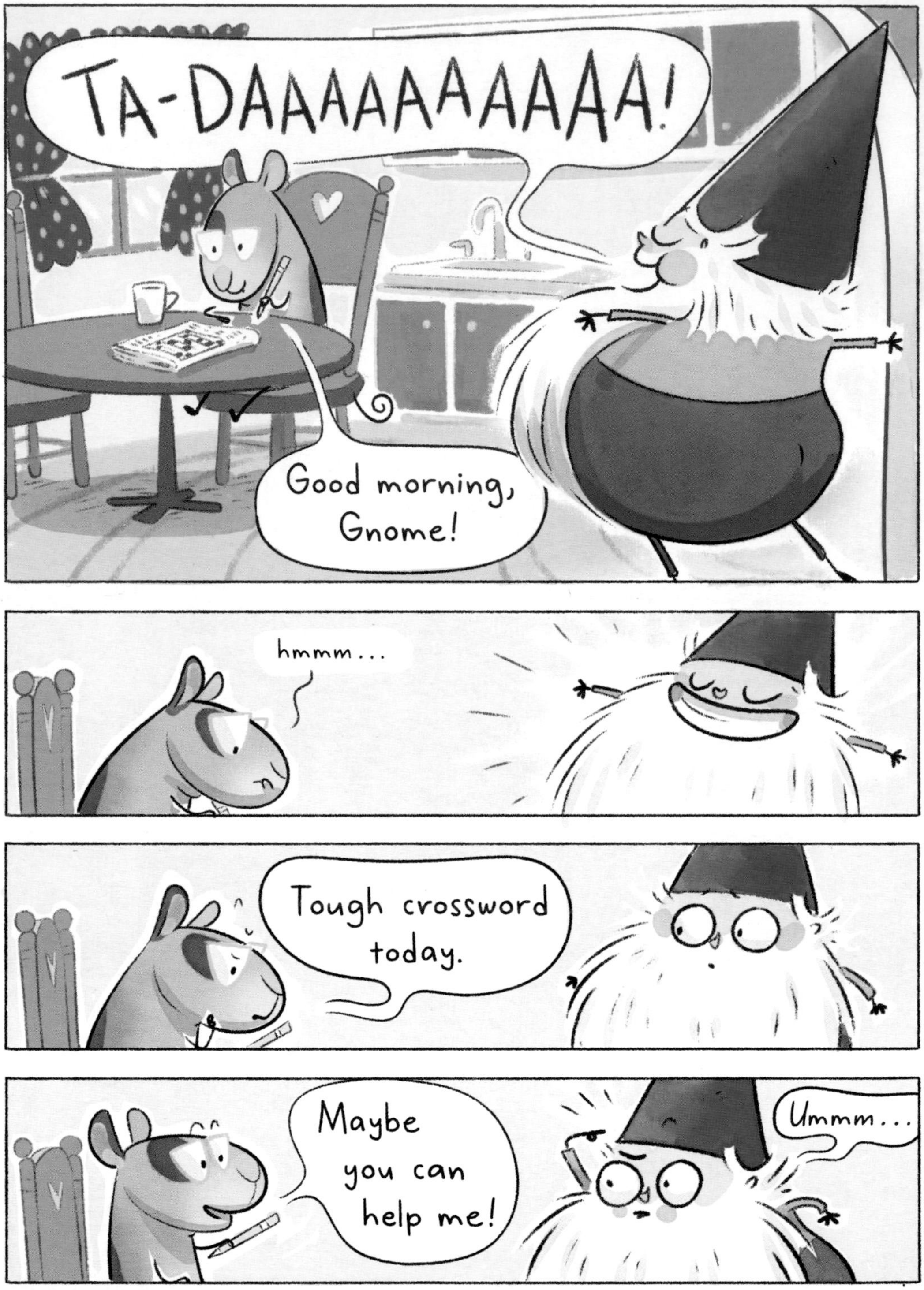
TA-DAAAAAAAAAA!
Good morning, Gnome!
hmmm...
Tough crossword today.
Maybe you can help me!
Ummm...

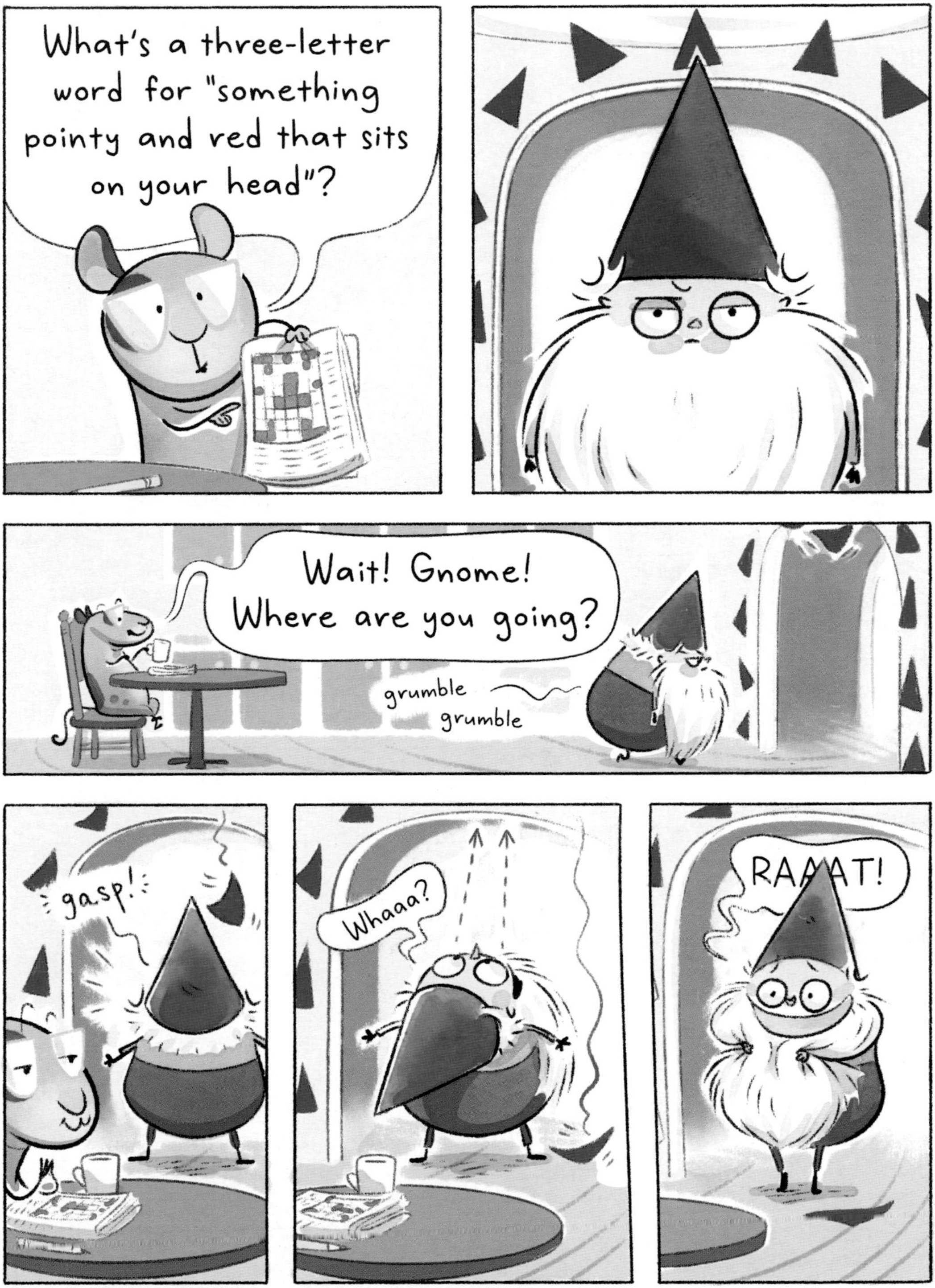
What's a three-letter word for "something pointy and red that sits on your head"?
Wait! Gnome! Where are you going?
grumble
grumble
gasp!
Whaaa?
RAAAT!

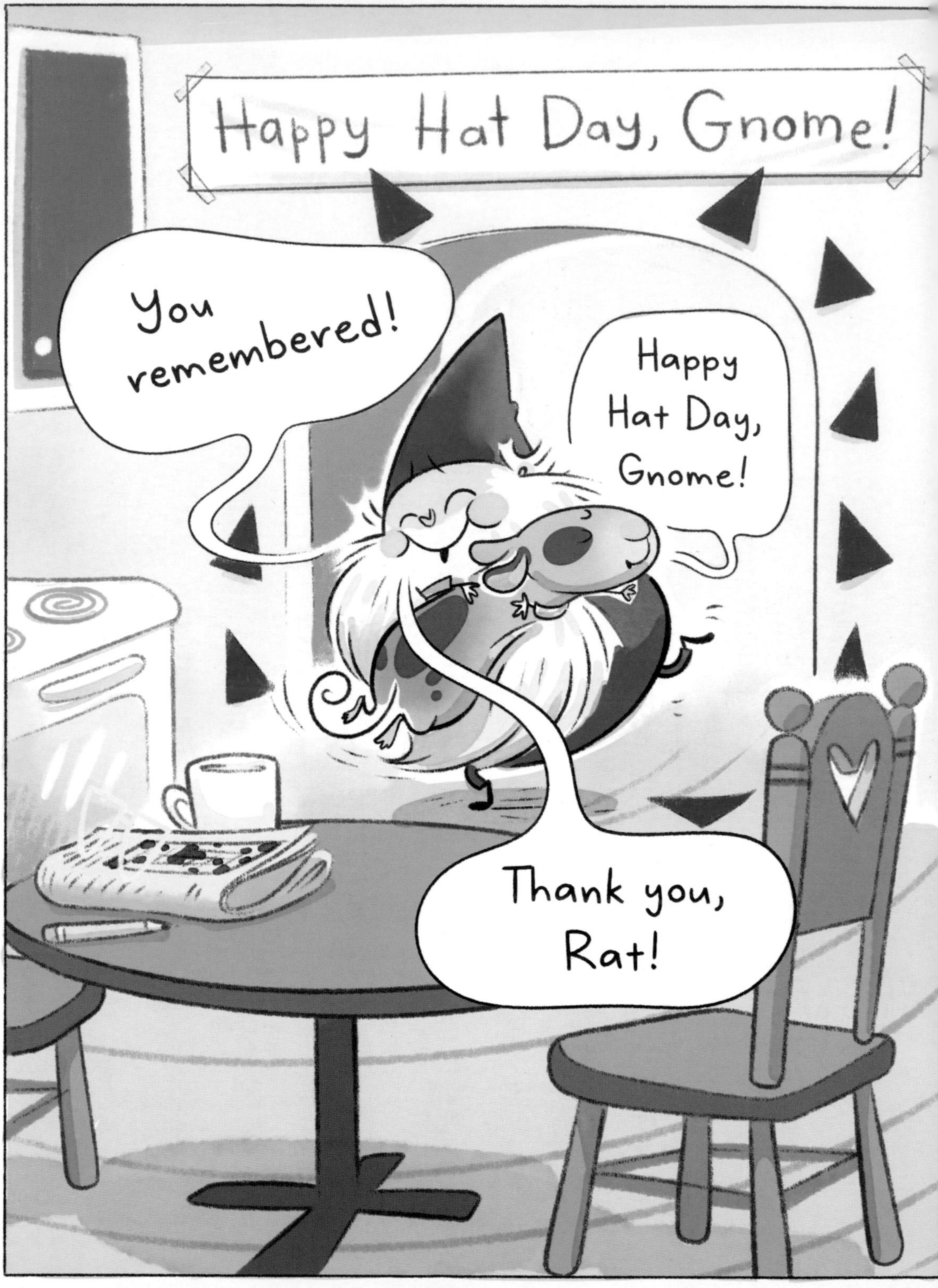
Happy Hat Day, Gnome!
You remembered!
Happy Hat Day, Gnome!
Thank you, Rat!

Happy Hat Day to you,
happy Hat Day to you,
happy Hat Day
dear Gno-ome,
happy Hat Day to
yoooooooouuuuuuu!

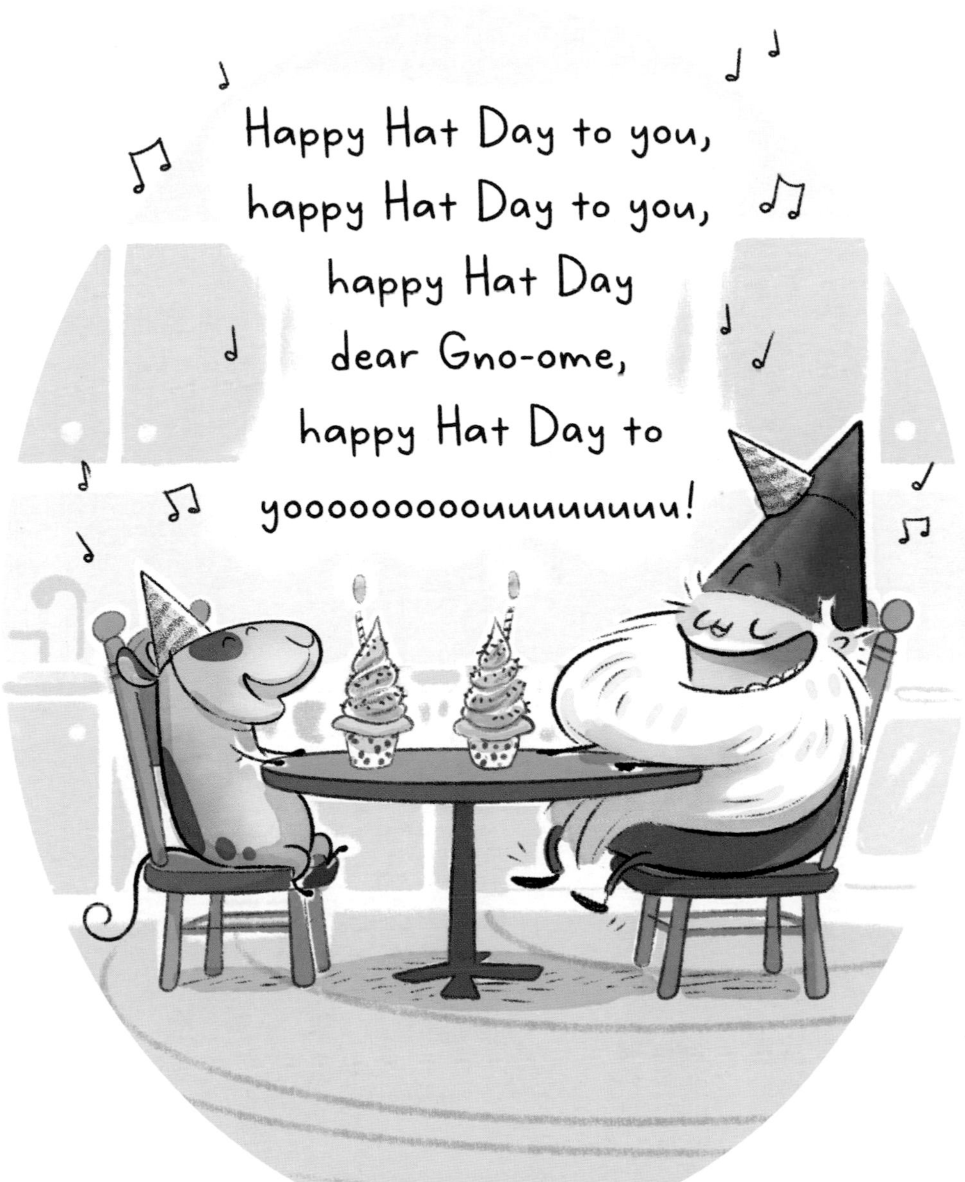

CHAPTER 2

Gnome Fits
in a Hat

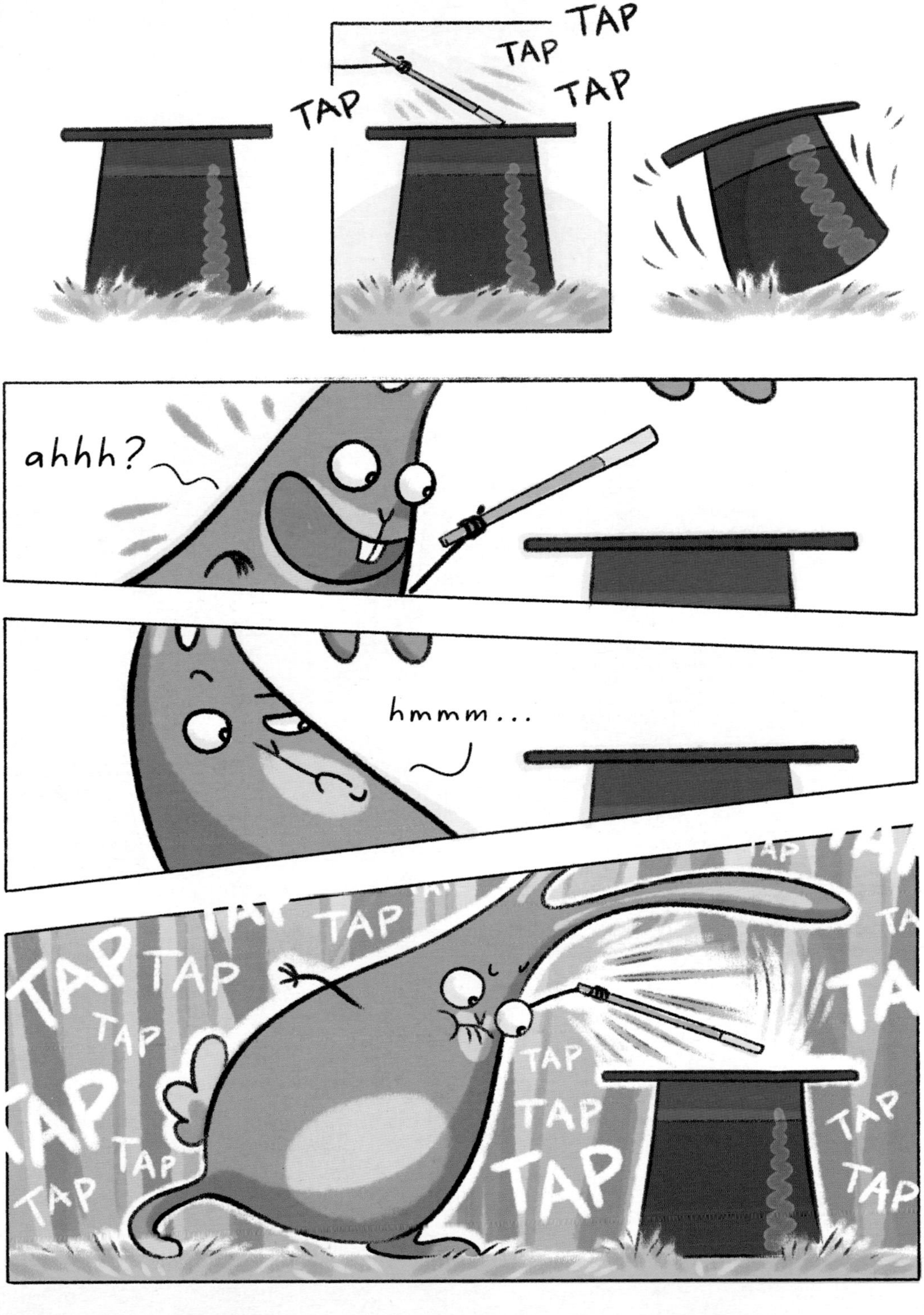

TAP
TAP
TAP
TAP
ahhh?
hmmm...
TAP TAP TAP TAP TAP TAP TAP TAP TAP TAP TAP TAP TAP

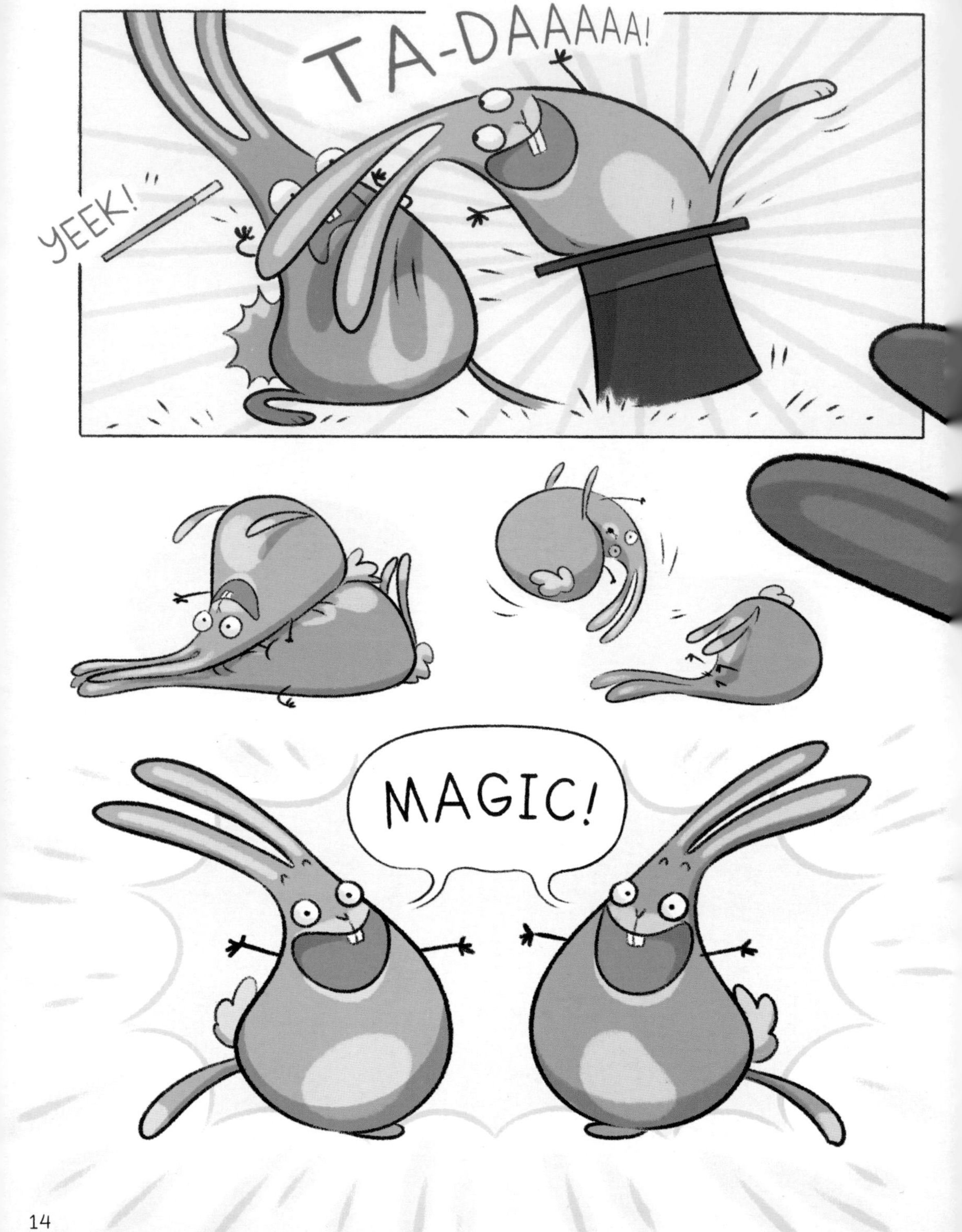
TA-DAAAAA!
YEEK!
MAGIC!

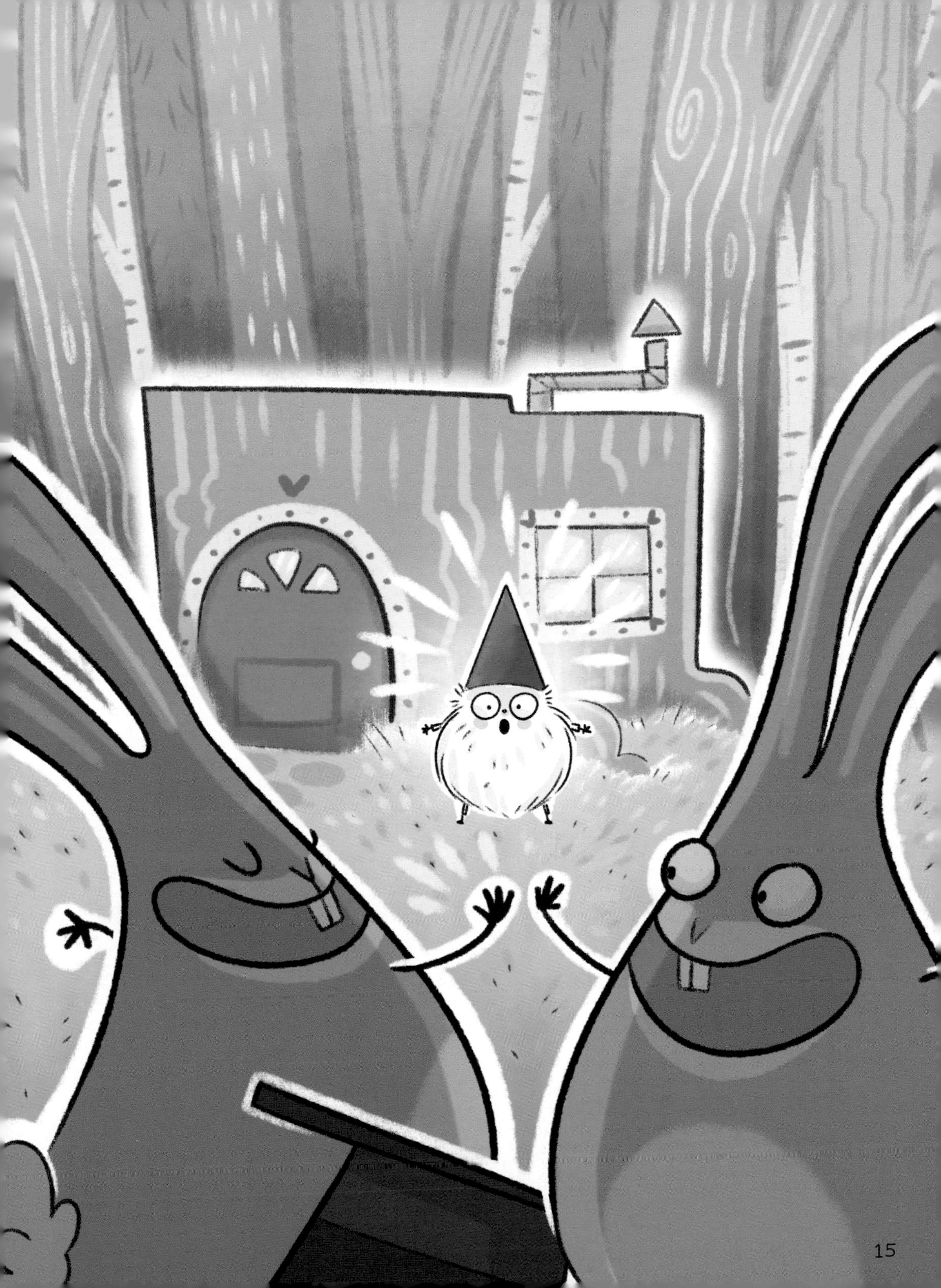

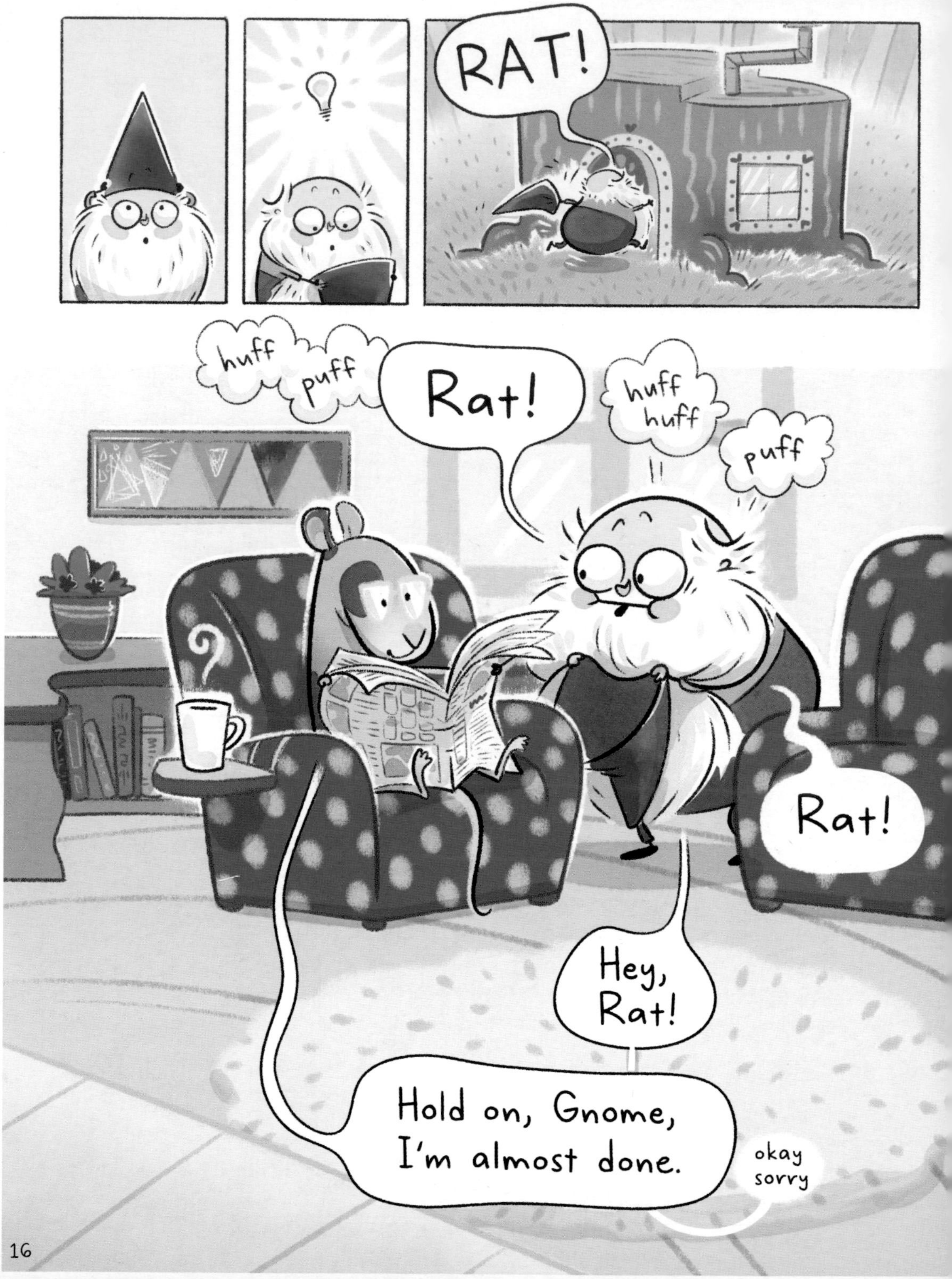
RAT!
huff puff
Rat!
huff huff
puff
Rat!
Hey, Rat!
Hold on, Gnome, I'm almost done.
okay sorry

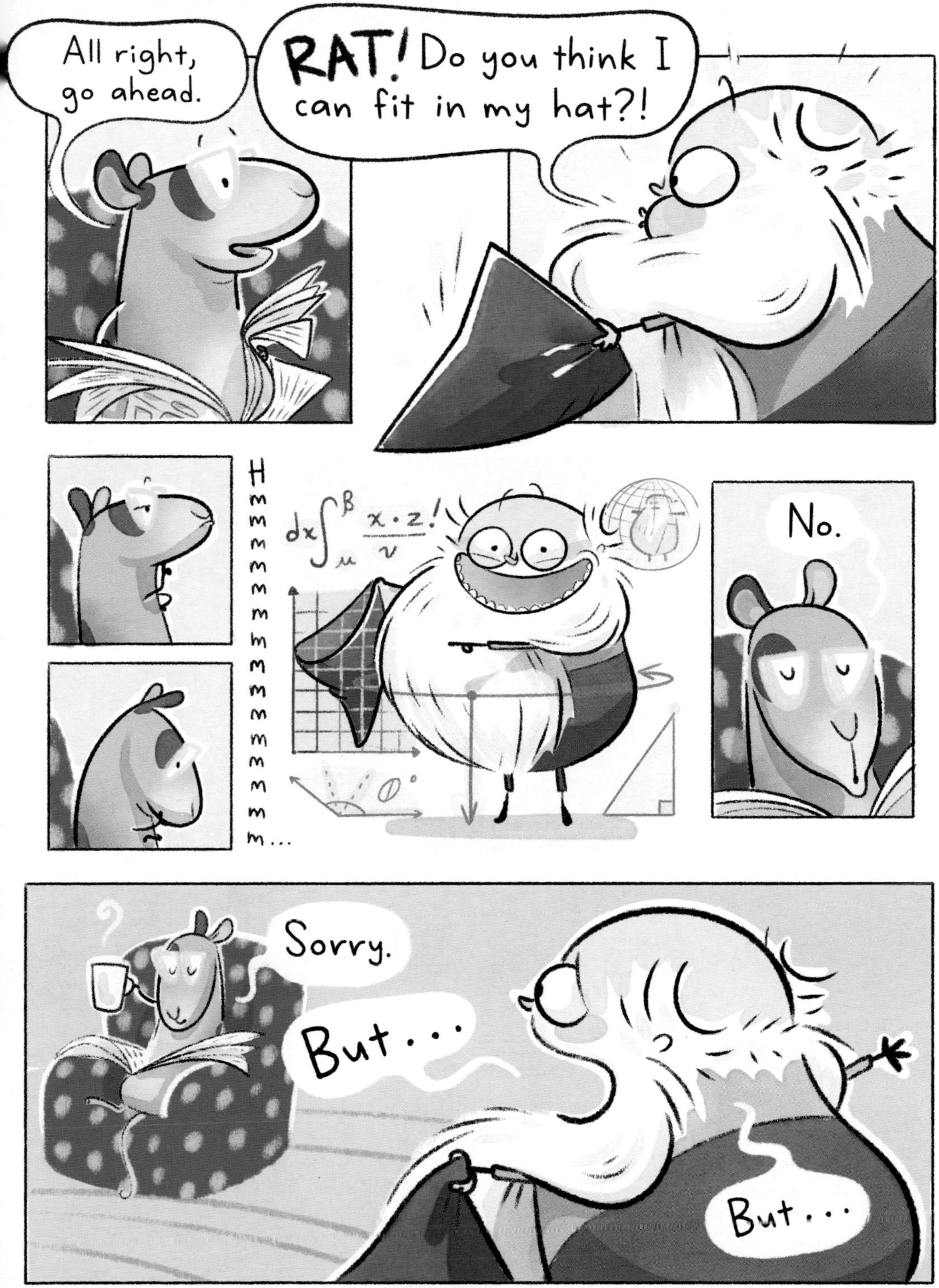
All right, go ahead.
RAT! Do you think I can fit in my hat?!
H m m m m m m m m m m m m m m m m...
No.
Sorry.
But...
But...

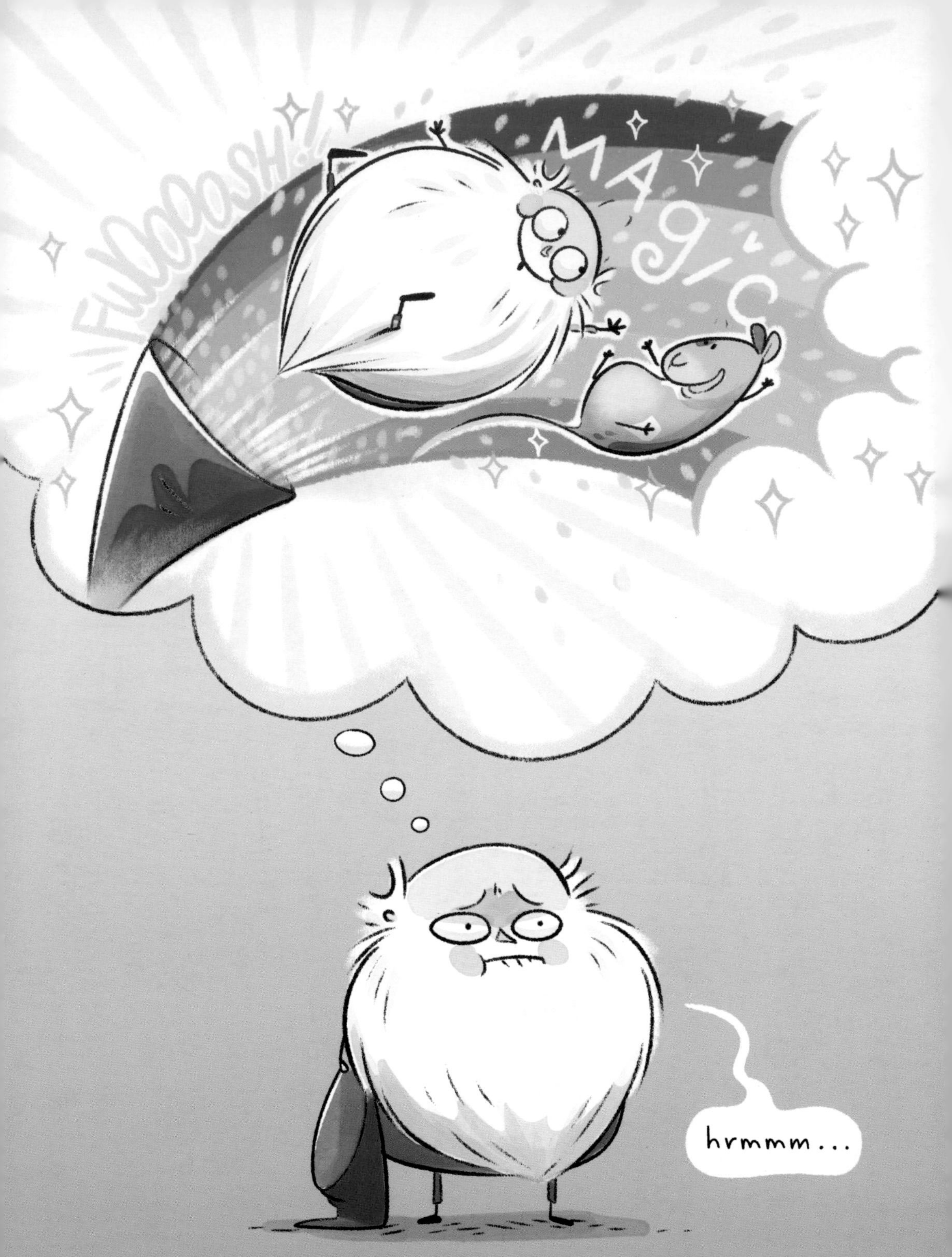
FWOOOOSH!!
MAGIC
hrmmm...

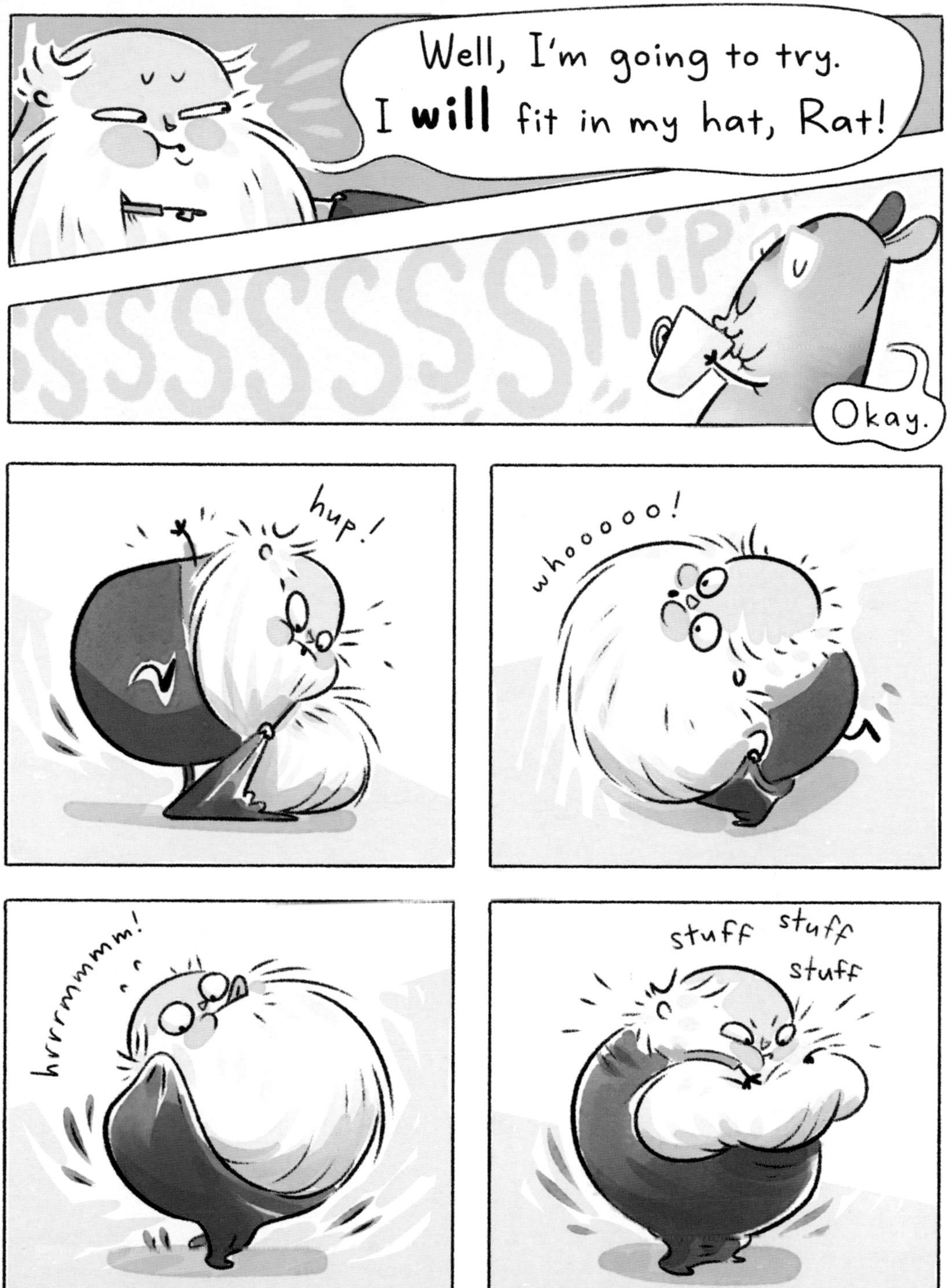
Well, I'm going to try.
I **will** fit in my hat, Rat!
SSSSSSSiiiiP...
Okay.
hup!
whoooooo!
hrrrmmmm!
stuff stuff
stuff

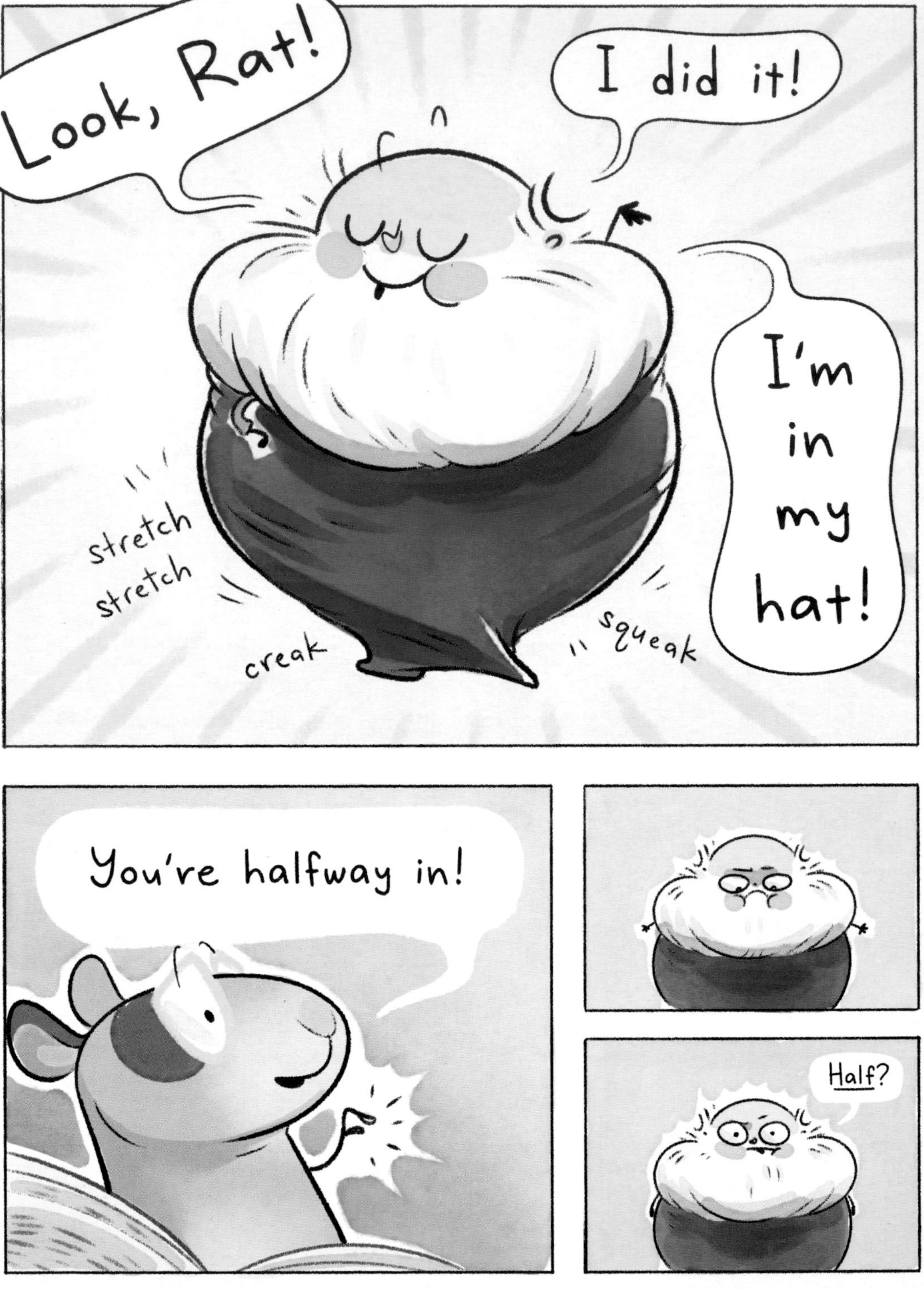
Look, Rat!
I did it!
I'm in my hat!
stretch stretch
creak
squeak
You're halfway in!
Half?

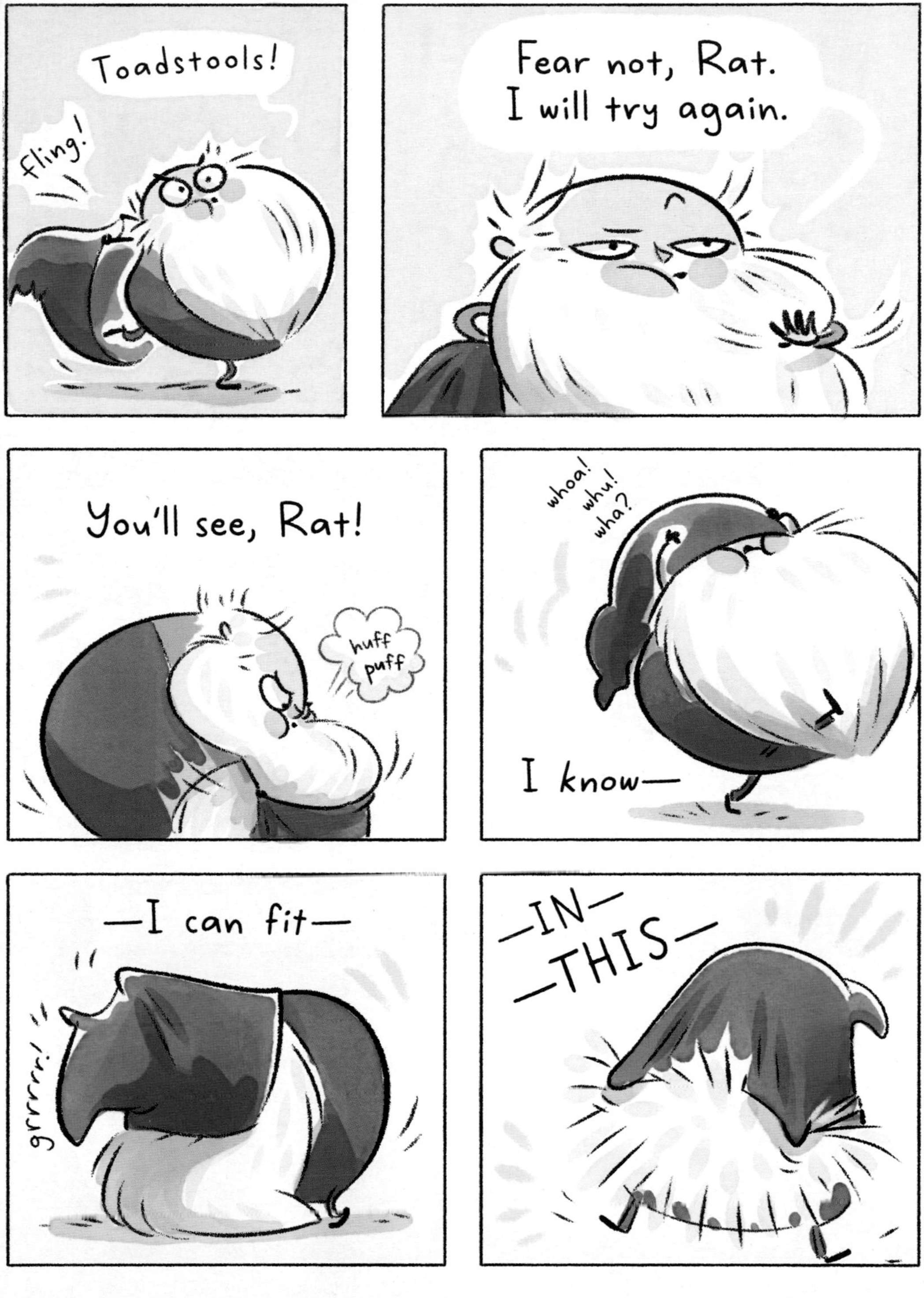
Toadstools!
fling!
Fear not, Rat. I will try again.
You'll see, Rat!
huff puff
whoa! whu! wha?
I know—
—I can fit—
grrrr!
—IN—
—THIS—

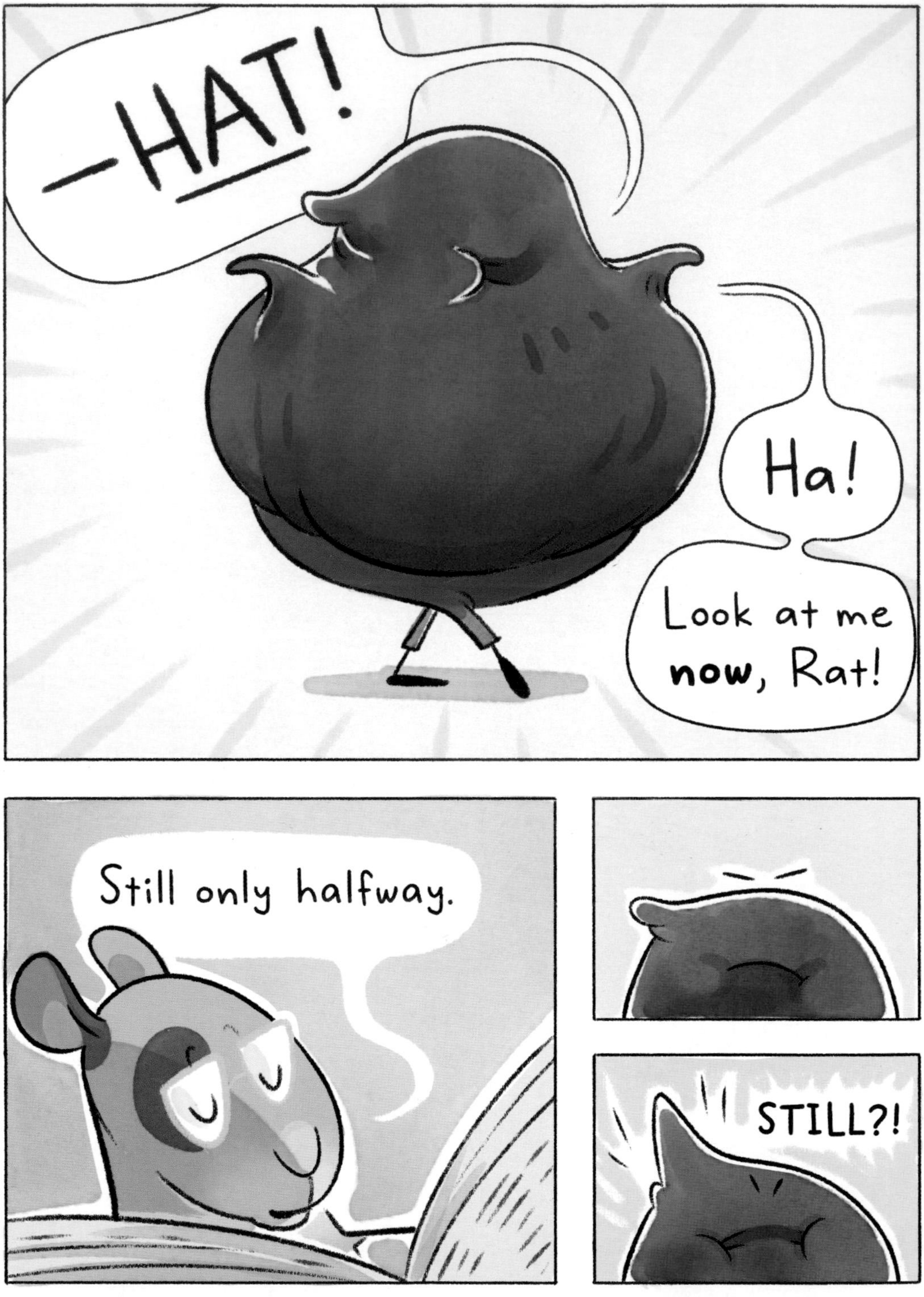

—HAT!
Ha!
Look at me **now**, Rat!
Still only halfway.
STILL?!

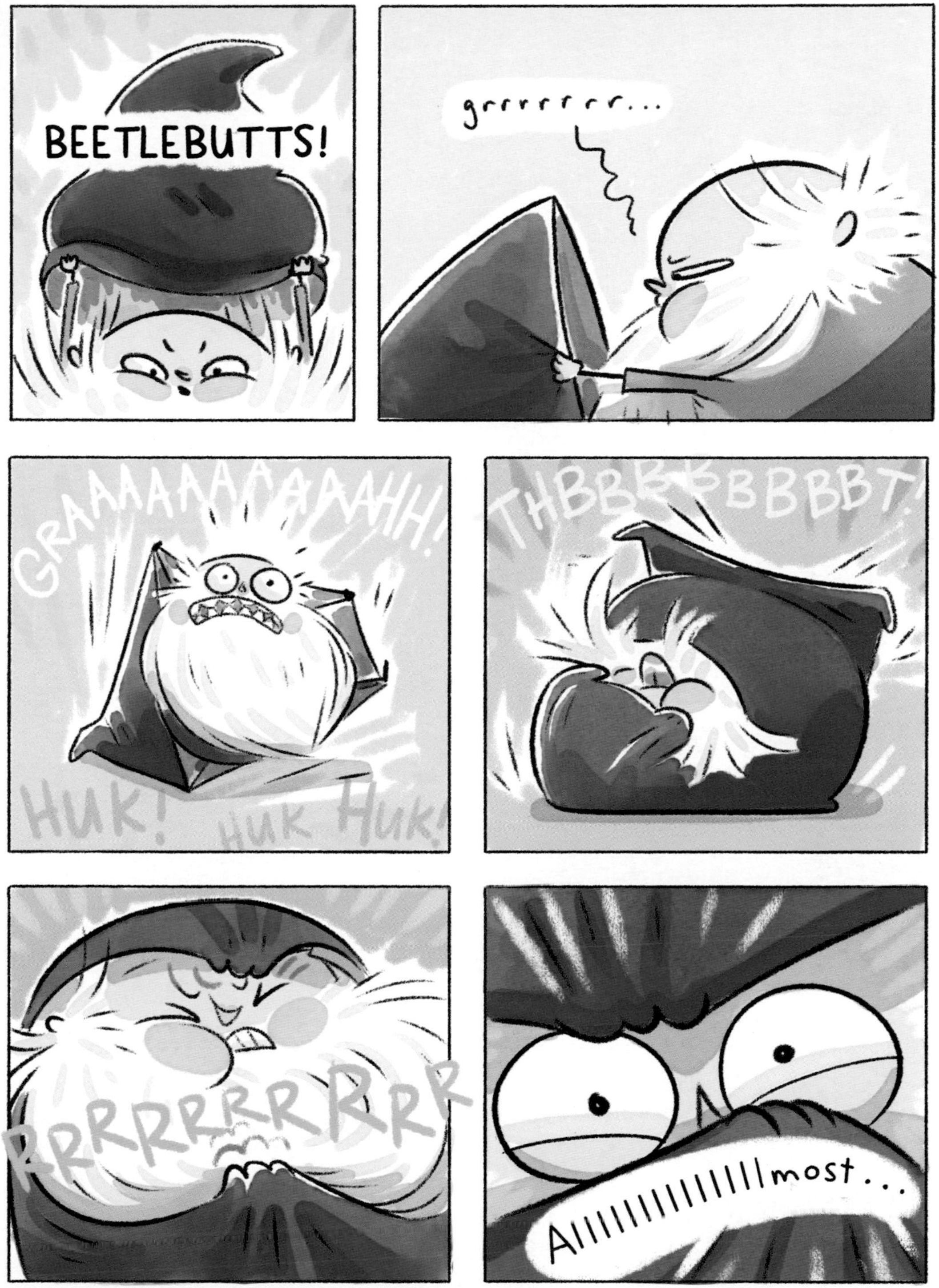
BEETLEBUTTS!
grrrrrrr...
GRAAAAAAAAAAHH!
HUK! HUK HUK!
THBBBBBBBBT!
RRRRRRRRRRR
AIIIIIIIIIIIIIIIlmost...

RAT!
I did it, Rat! I am ALL THE WAY inside my hat!
Now QUICK! Say some MAGIC WORDS, okay, Rat?

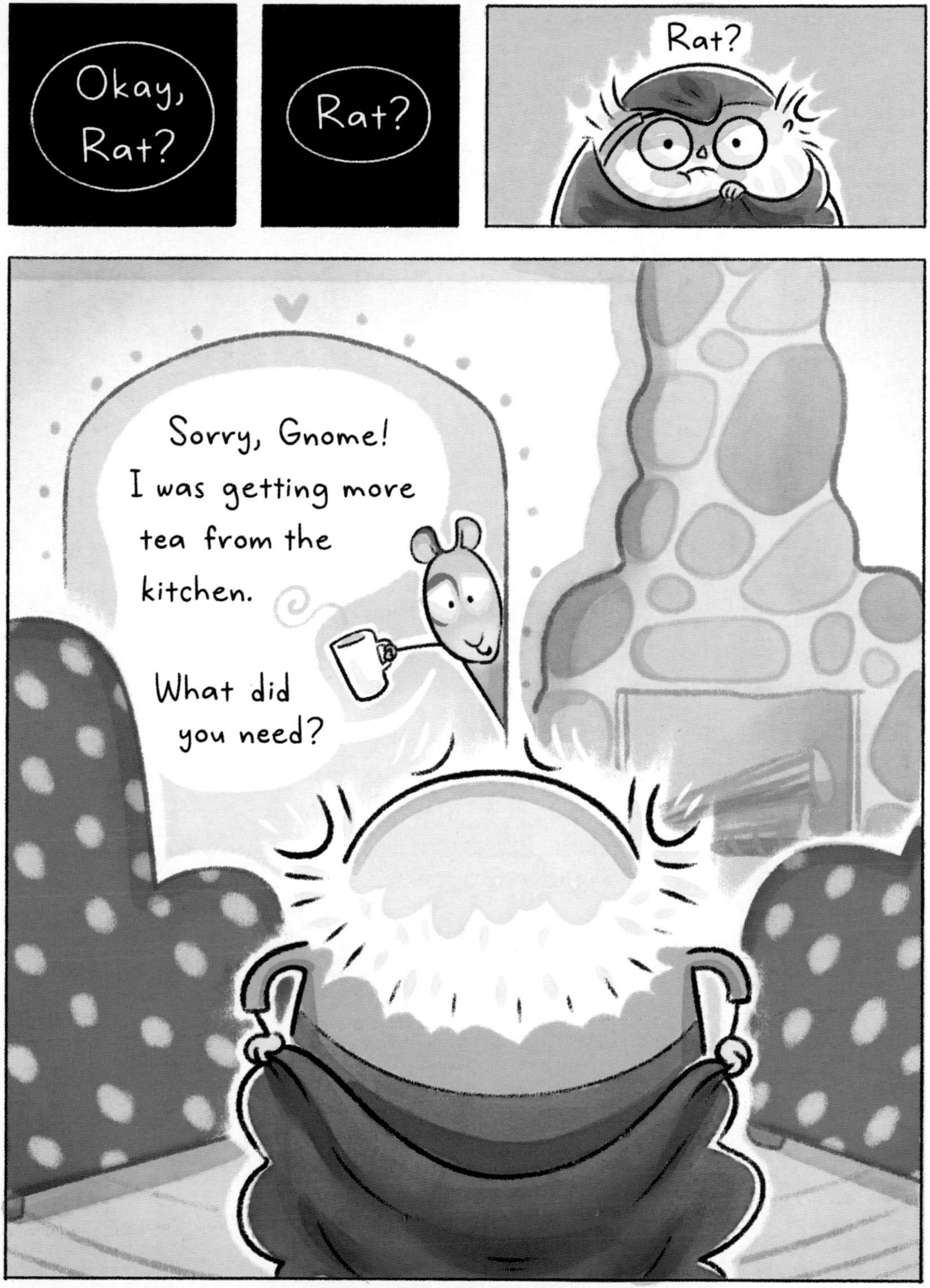
Okay, Rat?
Rat?
Rat?
Sorry, Gnome! I was getting more tea from the kitchen.
What did you need?

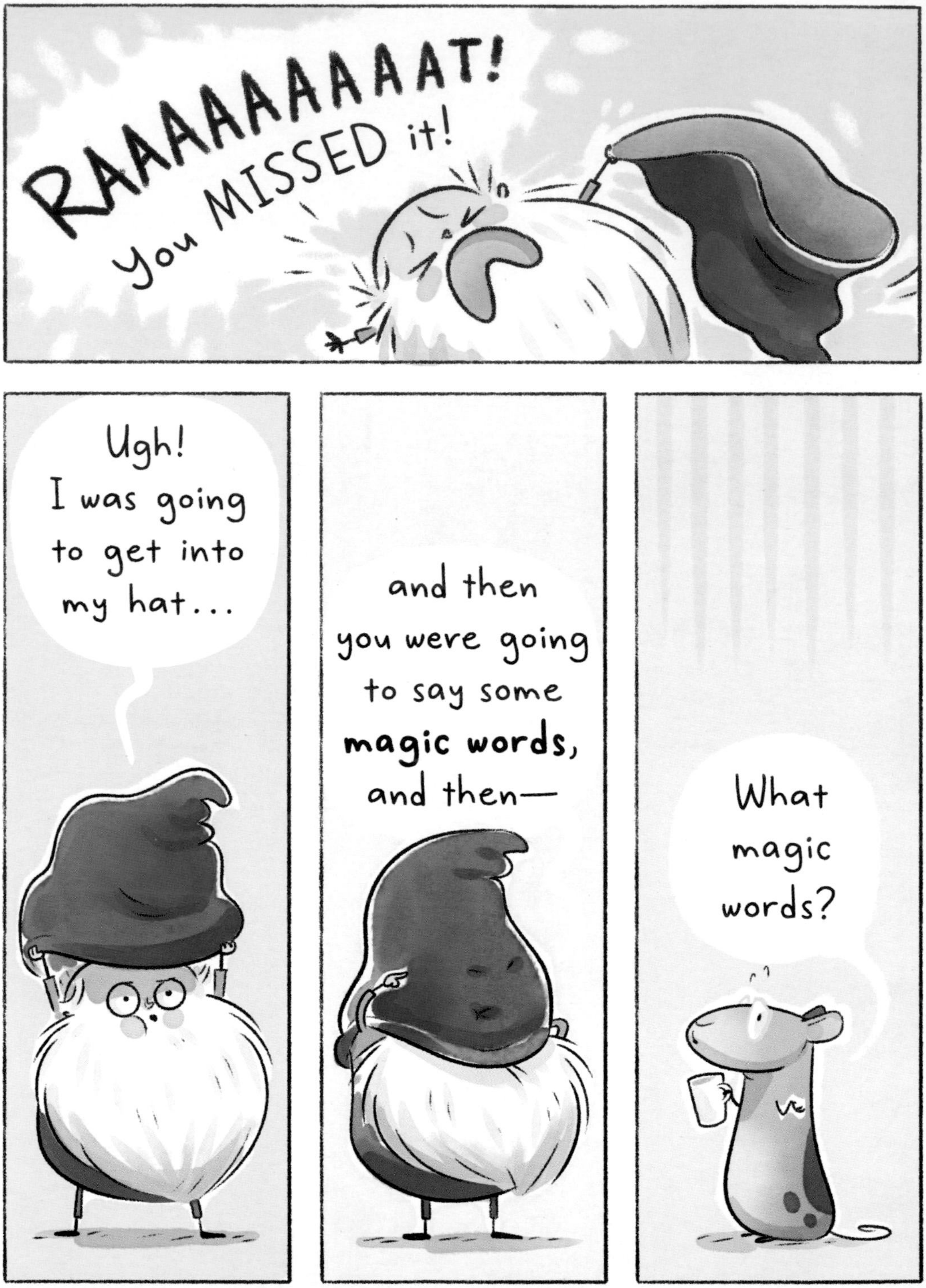
RAAAAAAAAAT!
You MISSED it!
Ugh! I was going to get into my hat...
and then you were going to say some **magic words**, and then—
What magic words?

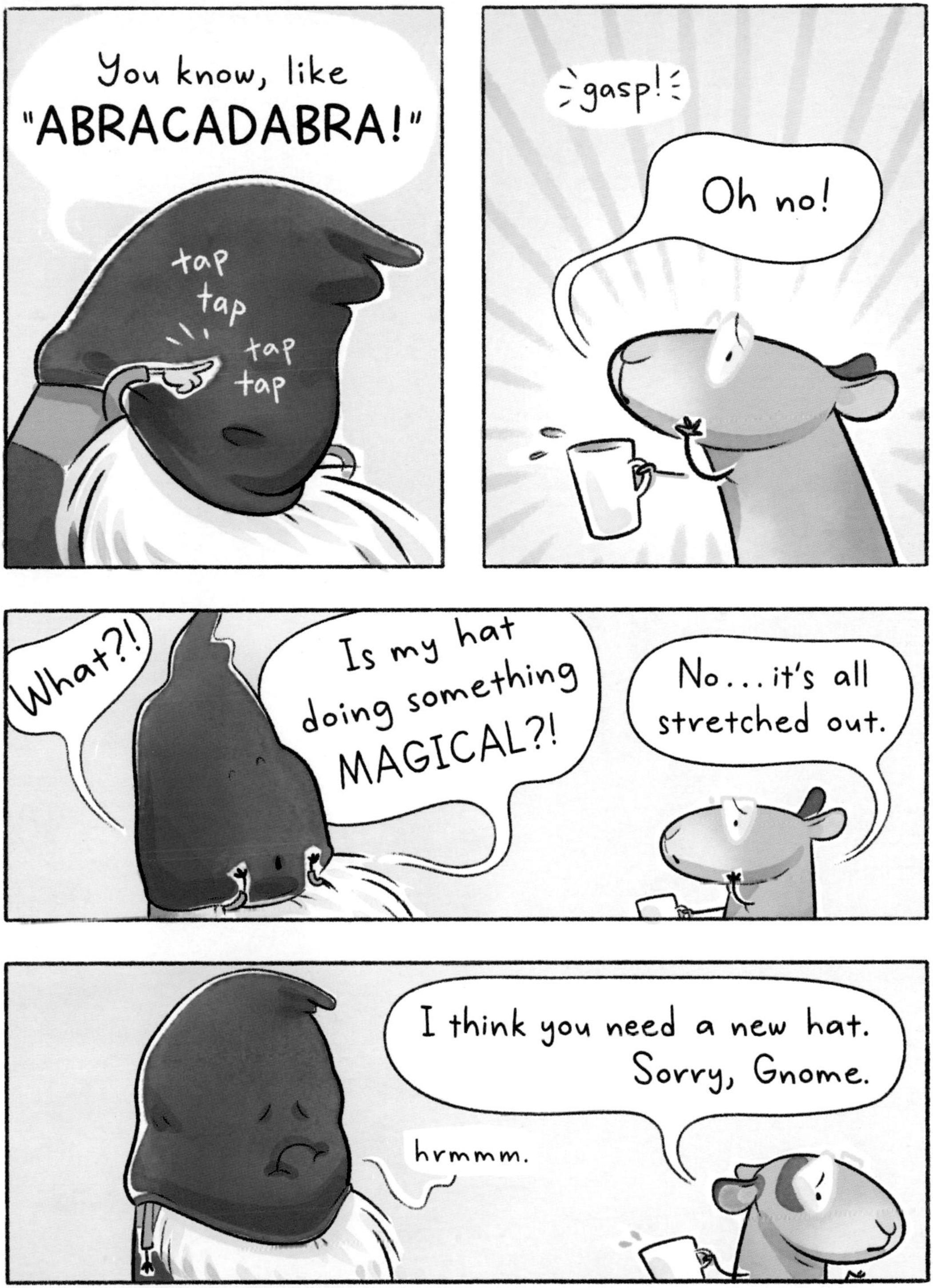
You know, like
"ABRACADABRA!"
tap
tap
tap
tap
gasp!
Oh no!
What?!
Is my hat doing something MAGICAL?!
No... it's all stretched out.
I think you need a new hat. Sorry, Gnome.
hrmmm.

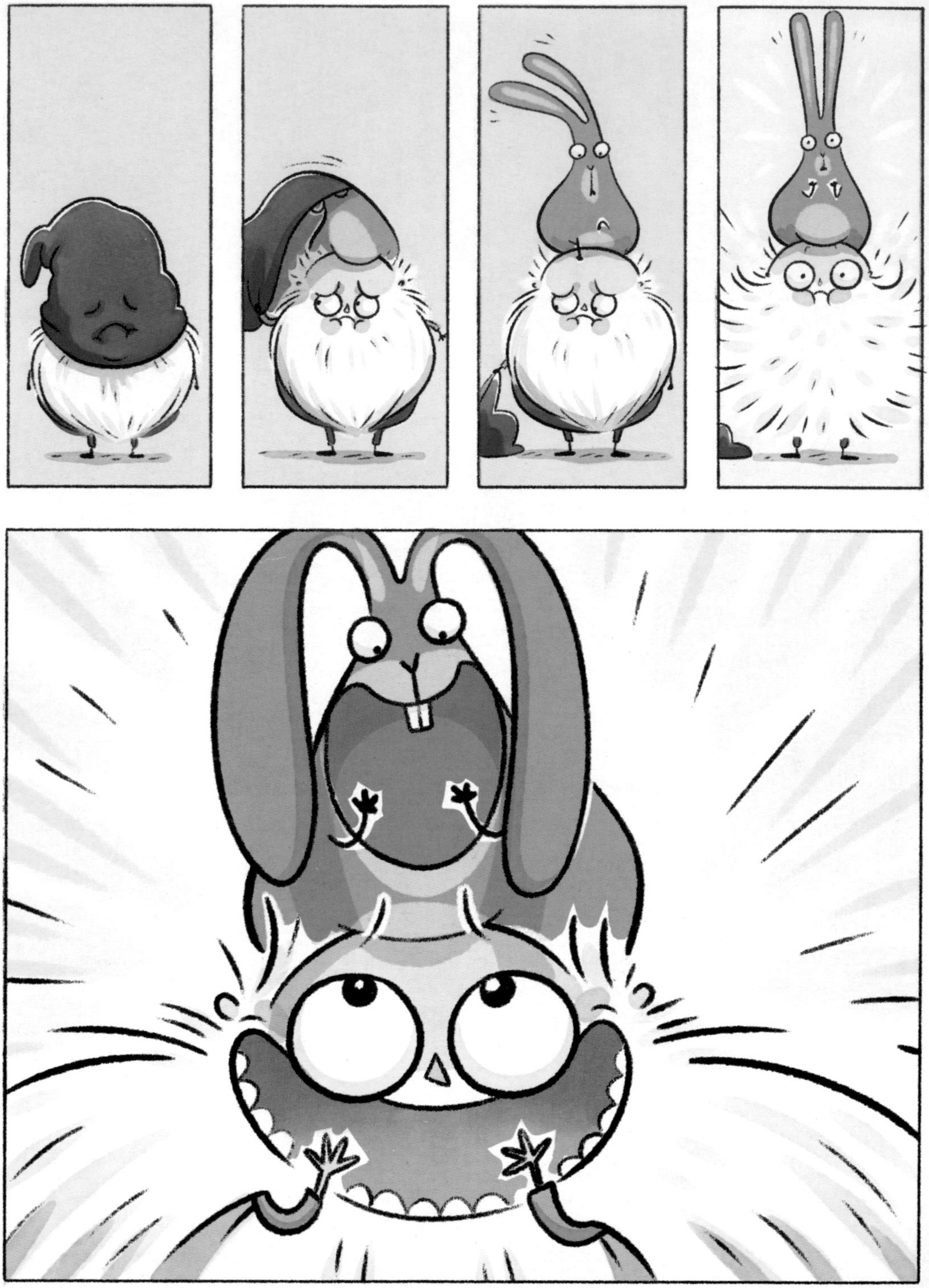

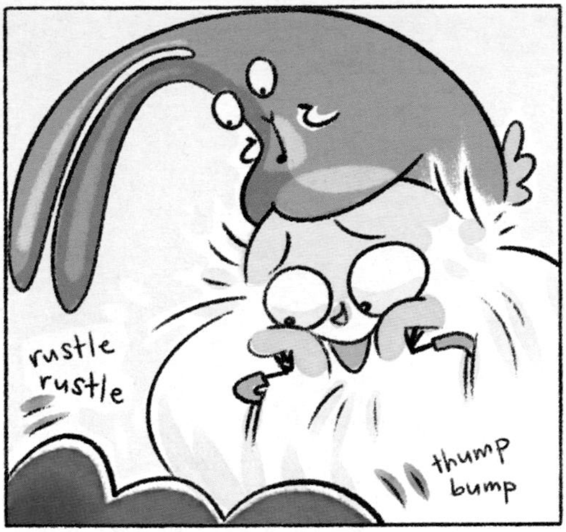
rustle
rustle
thump
bump

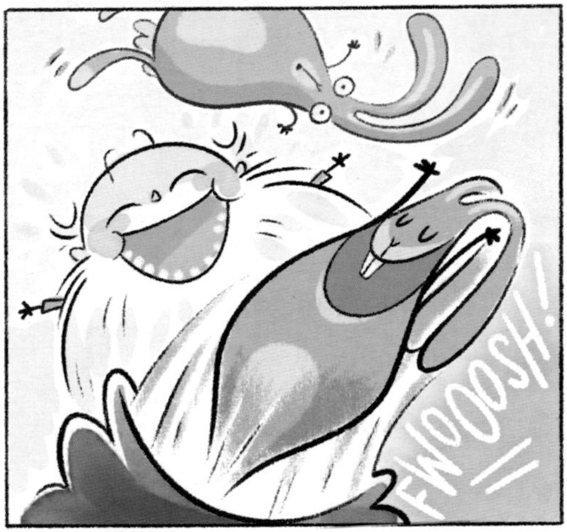
FWOOSH!

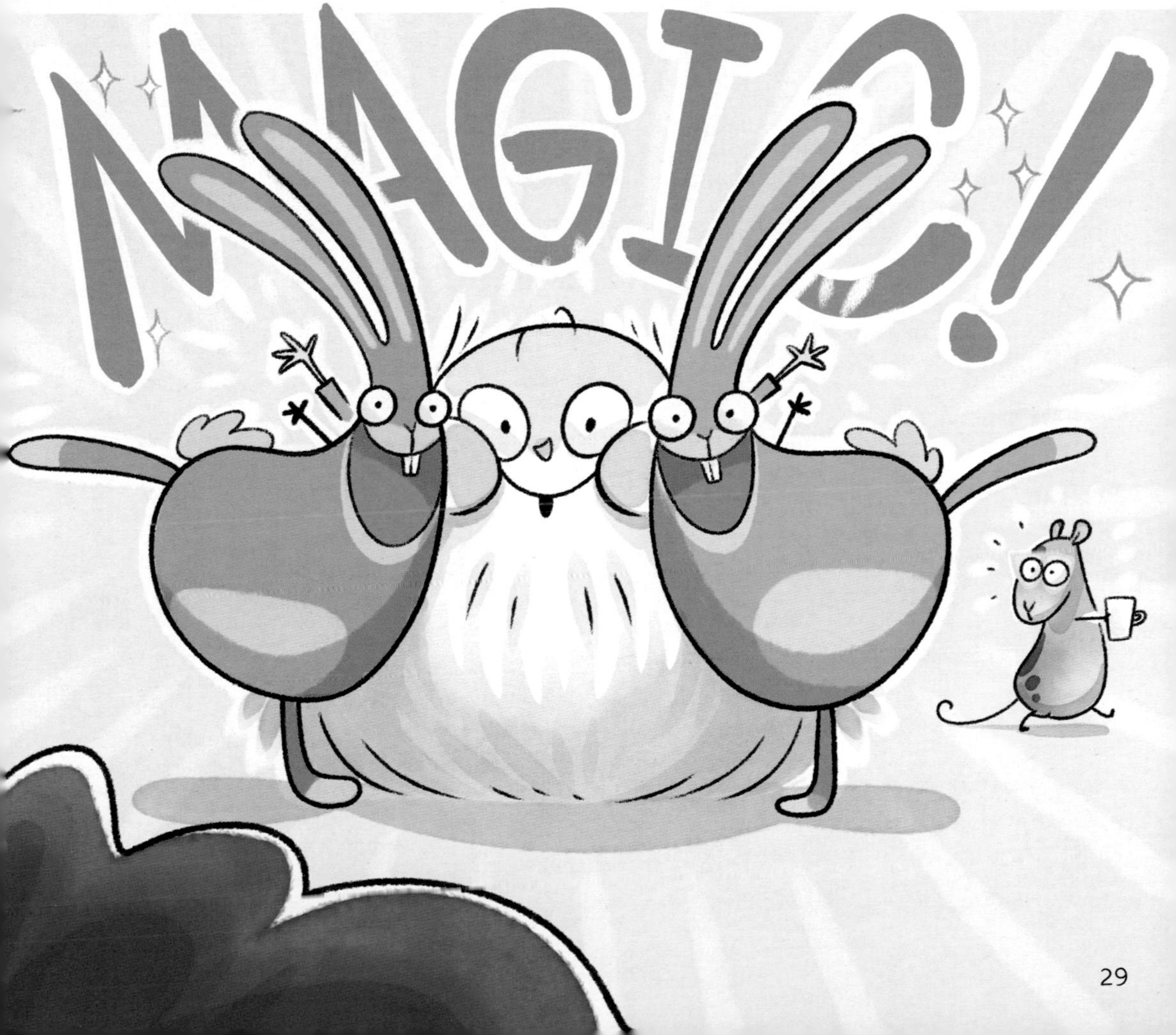
MAGIC!

CHAPTER 3

Gnome Grows His Hair

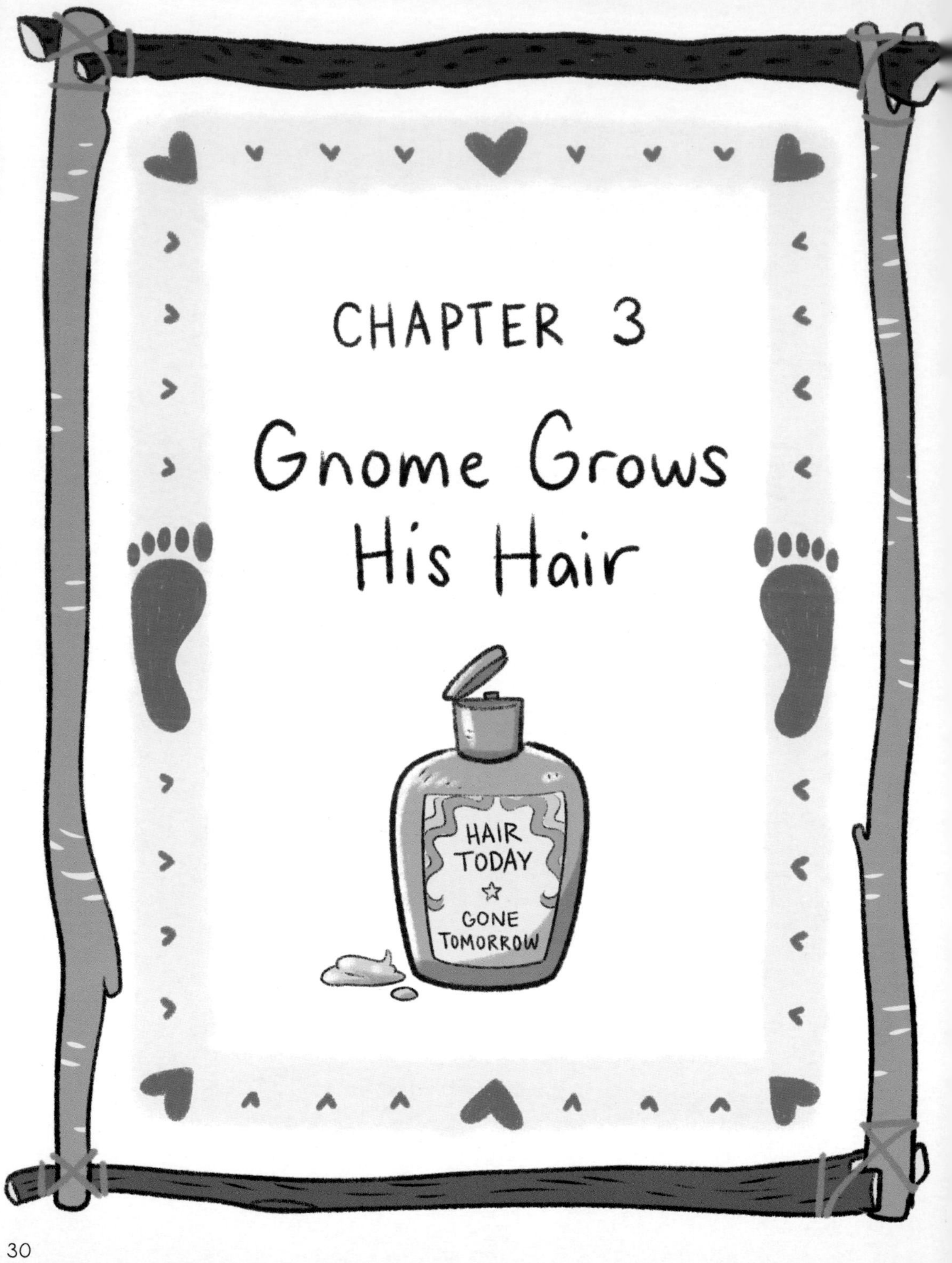
HAIR TODAY
☆
GONE TOMORROW

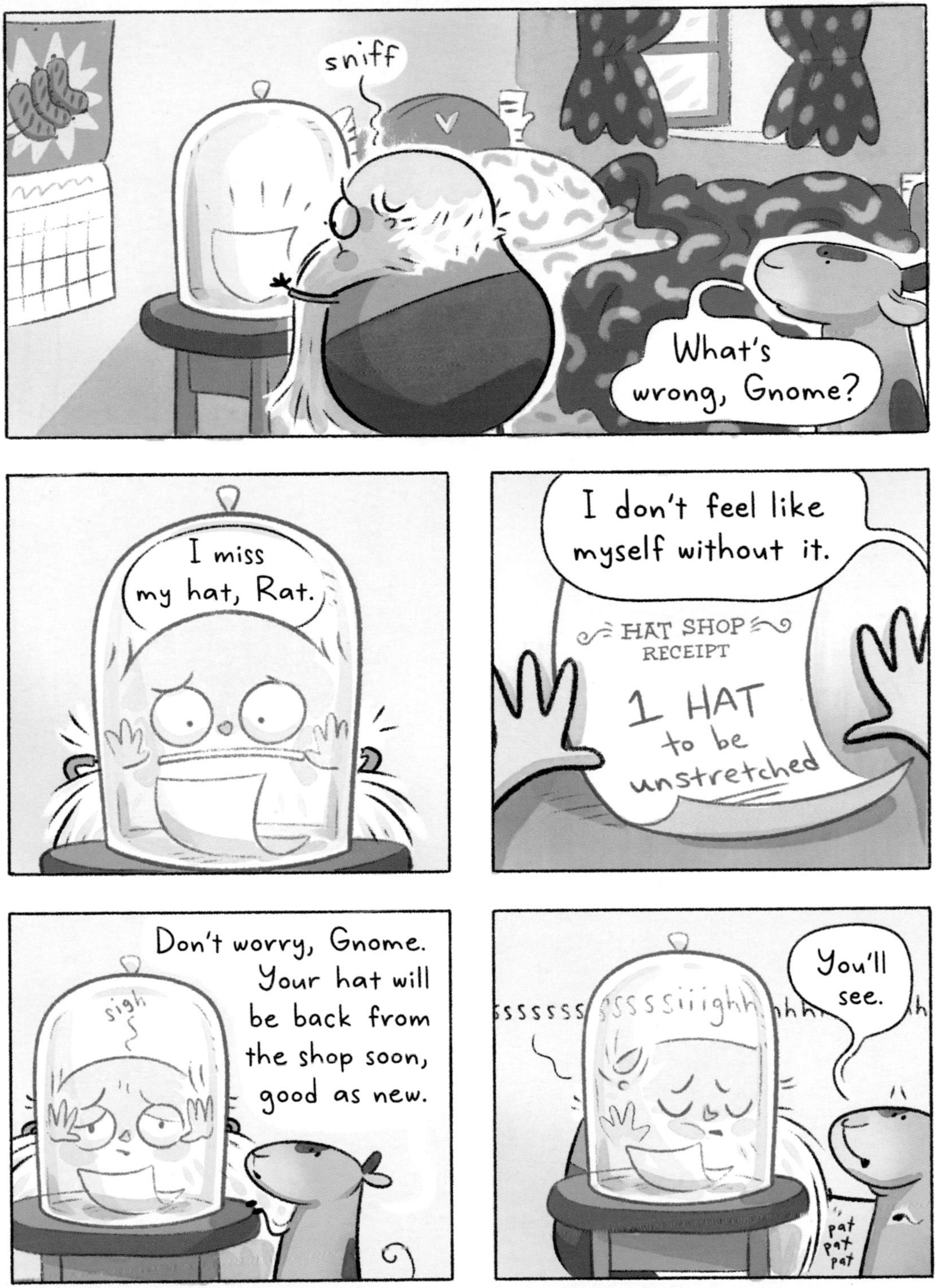
sniff
What's wrong, Gnome?
I miss my hat, Rat.
I don't feel like myself without it.
HAT SHOP
RECEIPT
1 HAT to be unstretched
Don't worry, Gnome. Your hat will be back from the shop soon, good as new.
sigh
sssssssssssiiighhhhhhh
You'll see.
pat pat pat

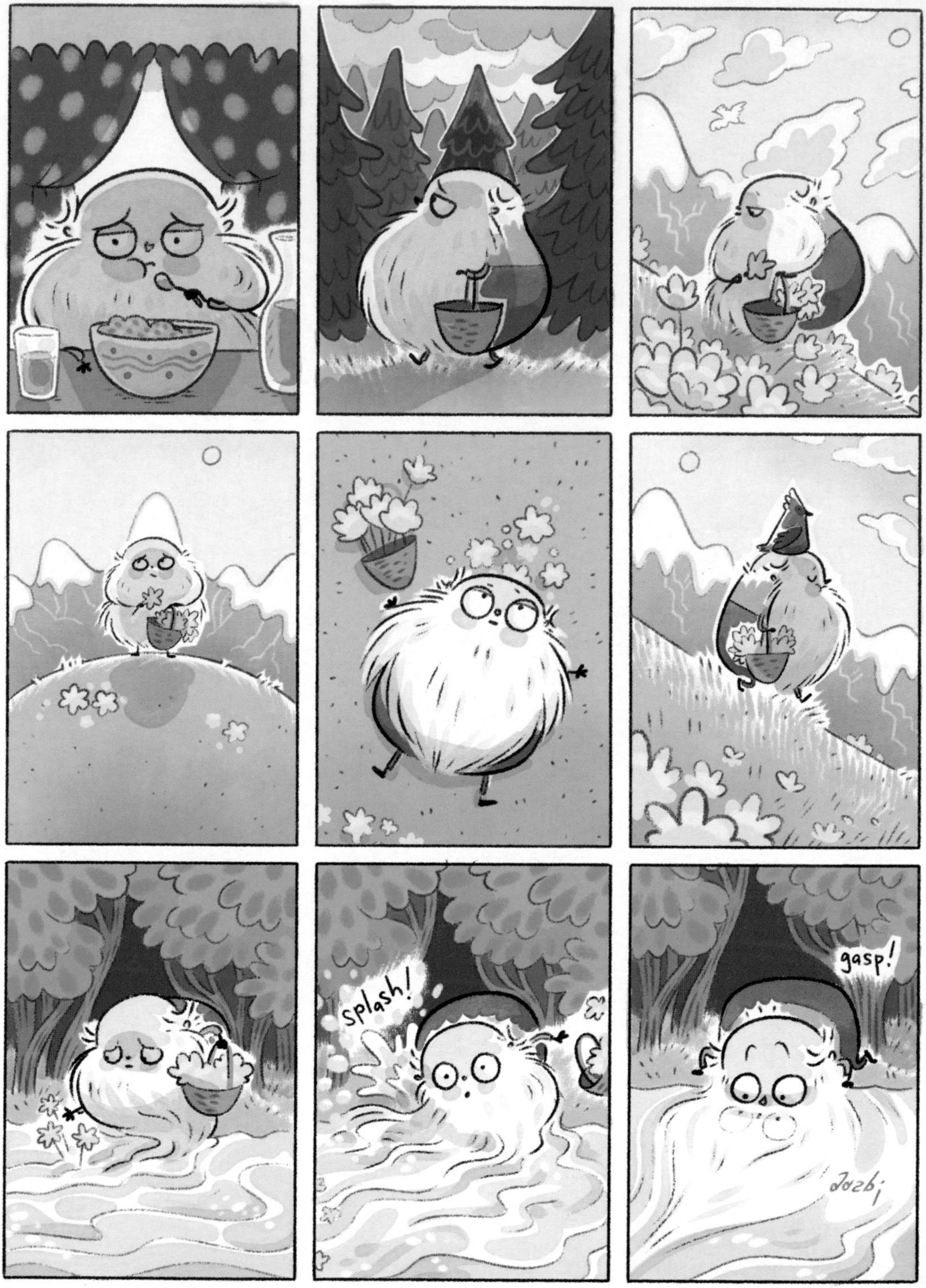
splash!
gasp!

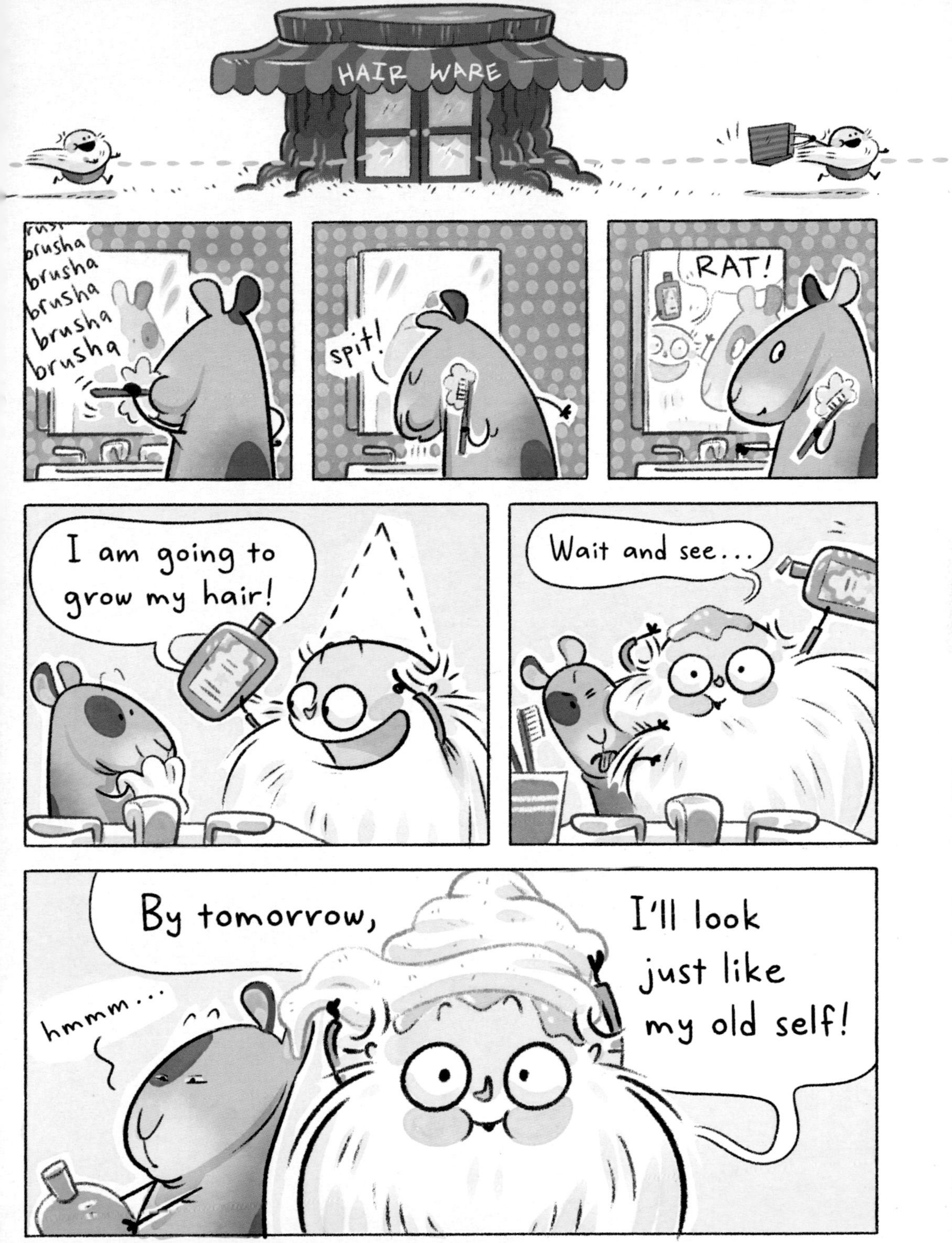
HAIR WARE
brusha
brusha
brusha
brusha
brusha
brusha
spit!
RAT!
I am going to grow my hair!
Wait and see...
By tomorrow,
I'll look just like my old self!
hmmm...

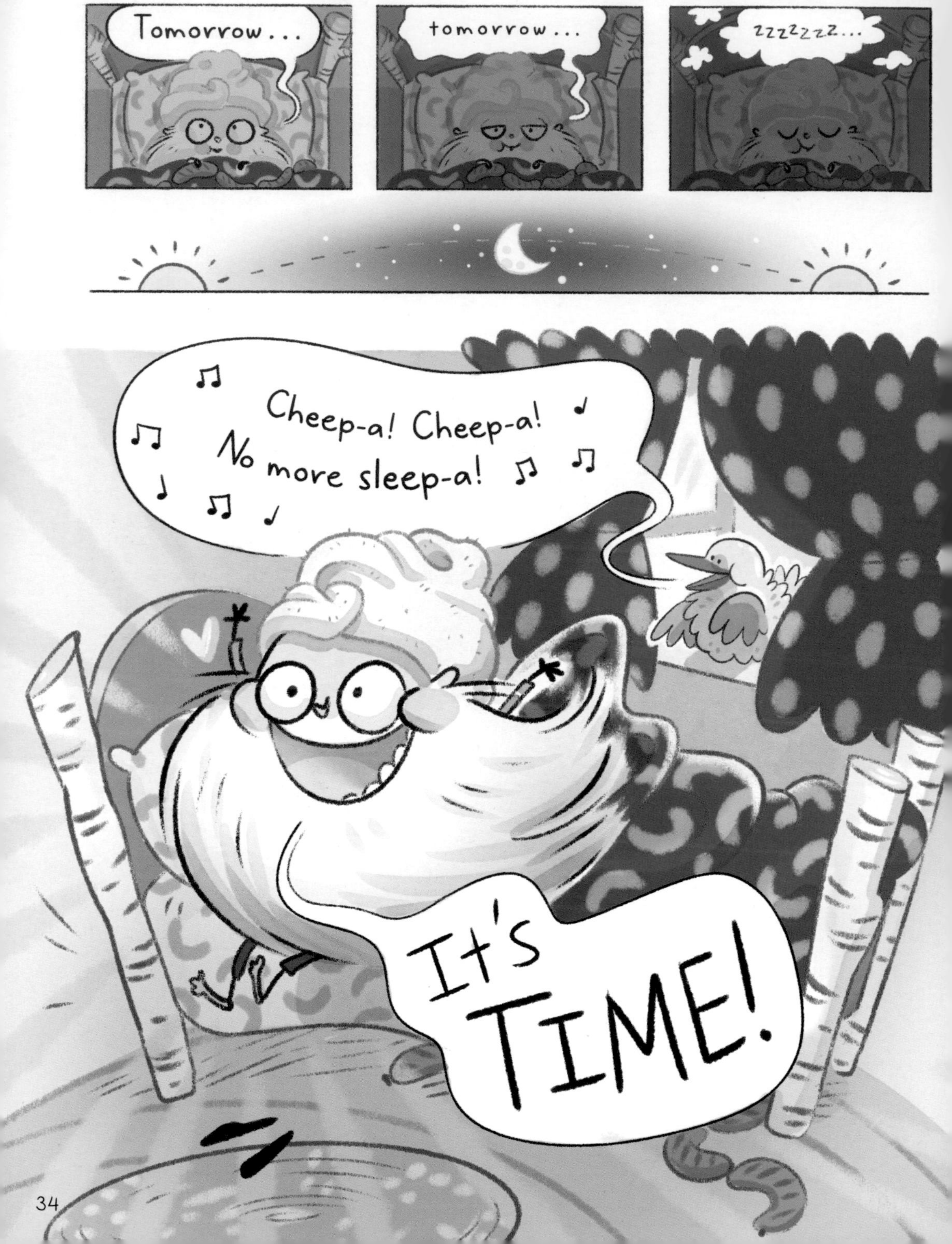
Tomorrow...
tomorrow...
zzzzzzz...
Cheep-a! Cheep-a! No more sleep-a!
It's TIME!

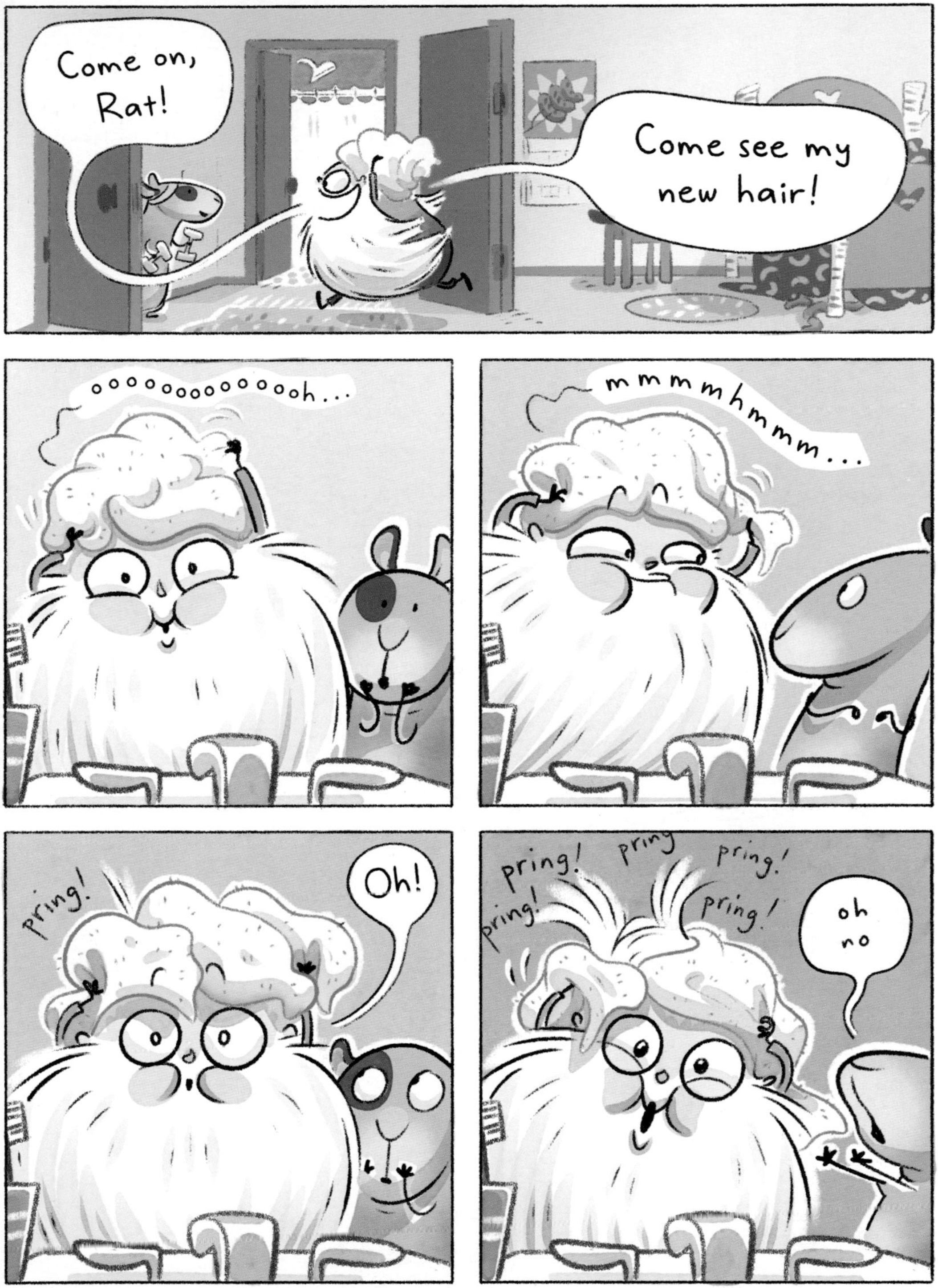
Come on, Rat!
Come see my new hair!
ooooooooooooh...
mmmmhmmmm...
pring!
Oh!
pring!
pring
pring!
pring!
pring!
oh no

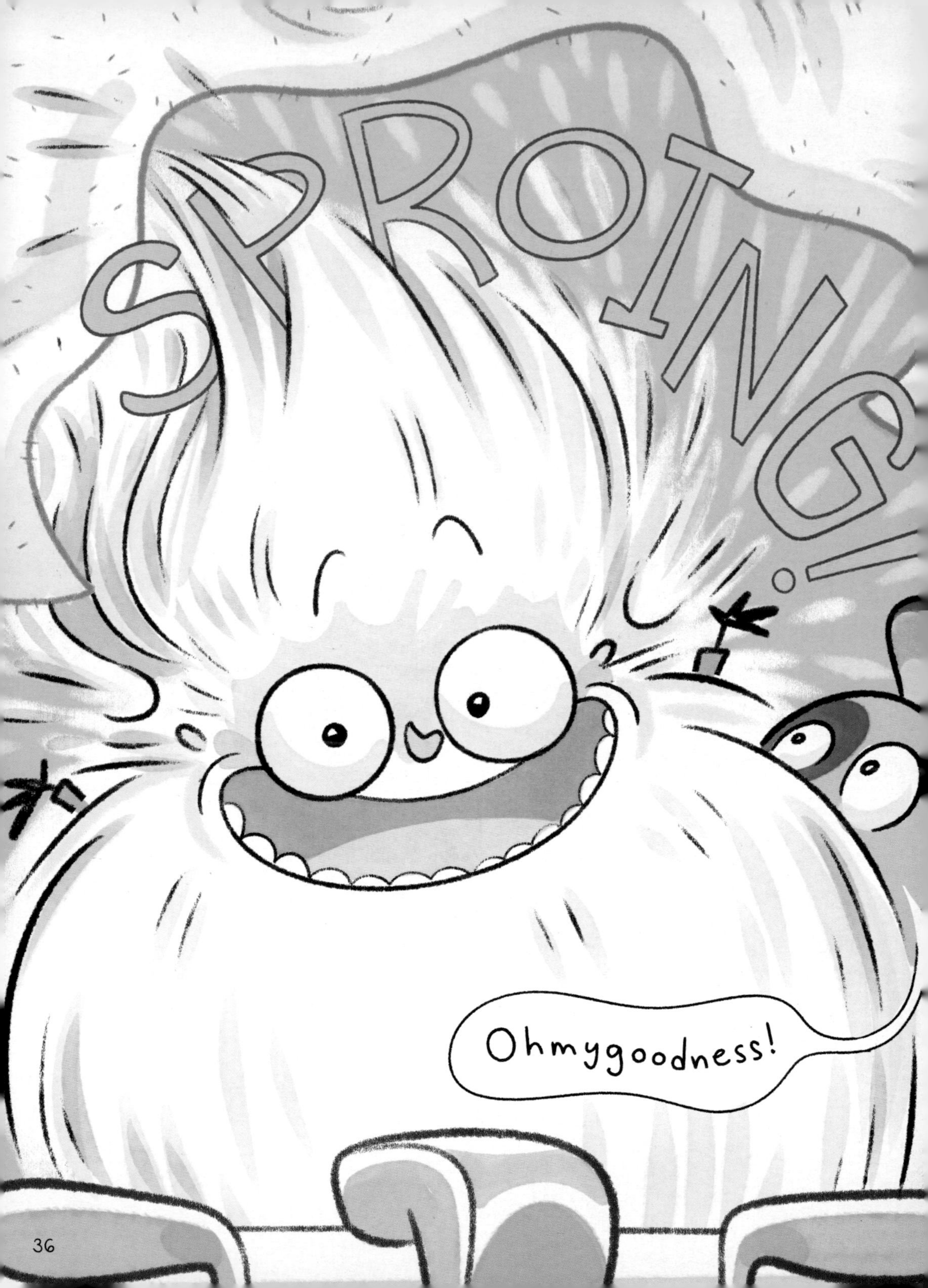
SPROING!
Ohmygoodness!

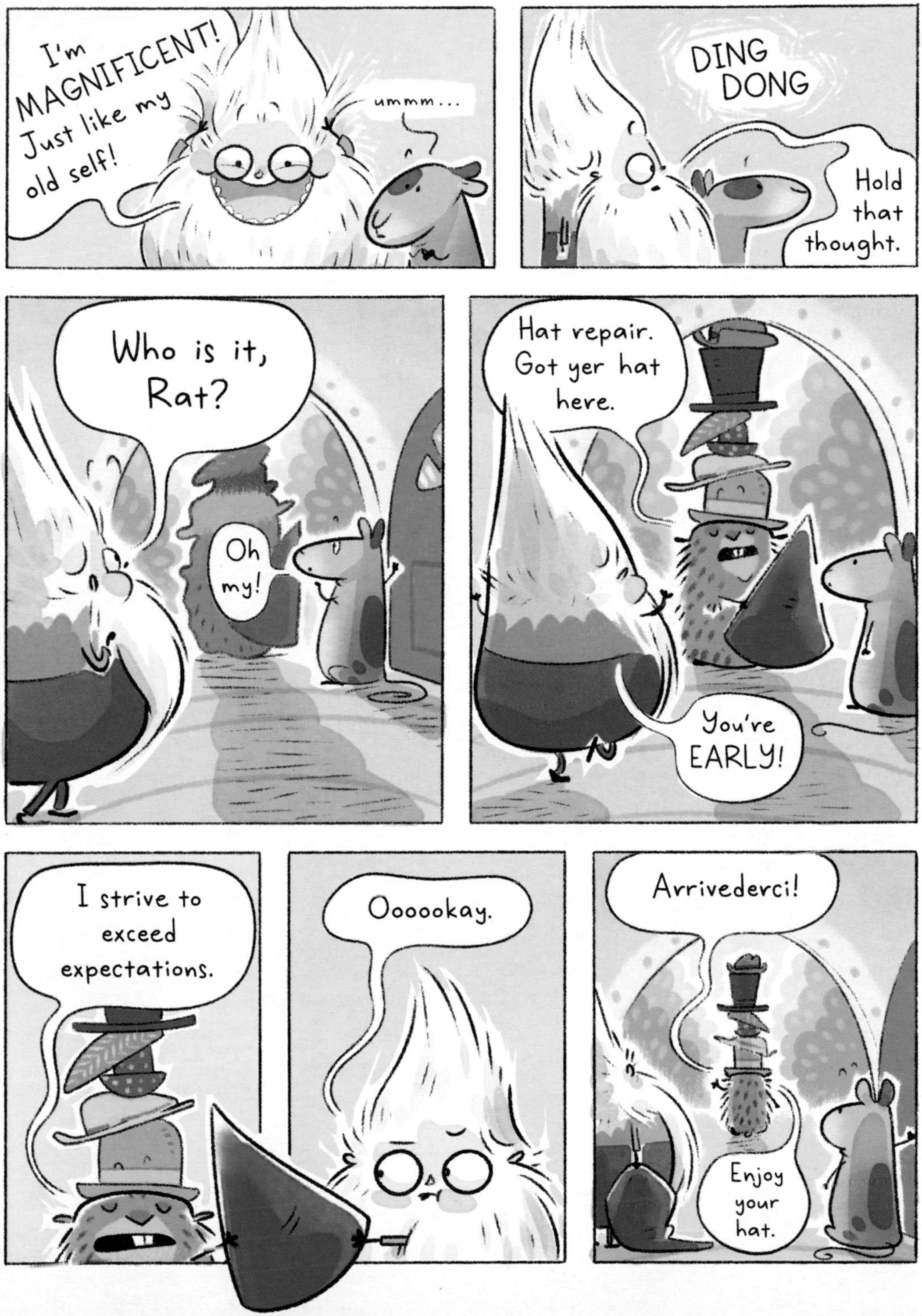
I'm MAGNIFICENT! Just like my old self!
ummm...
DING DONG
Hold that thought.
Who is it, Rat?
Oh my!
Hat repair. Got yer hat here.
You're EARLY!
I strive to exceed expectations.
Oooookay.
Arrivederci!
Enjoy your hat.

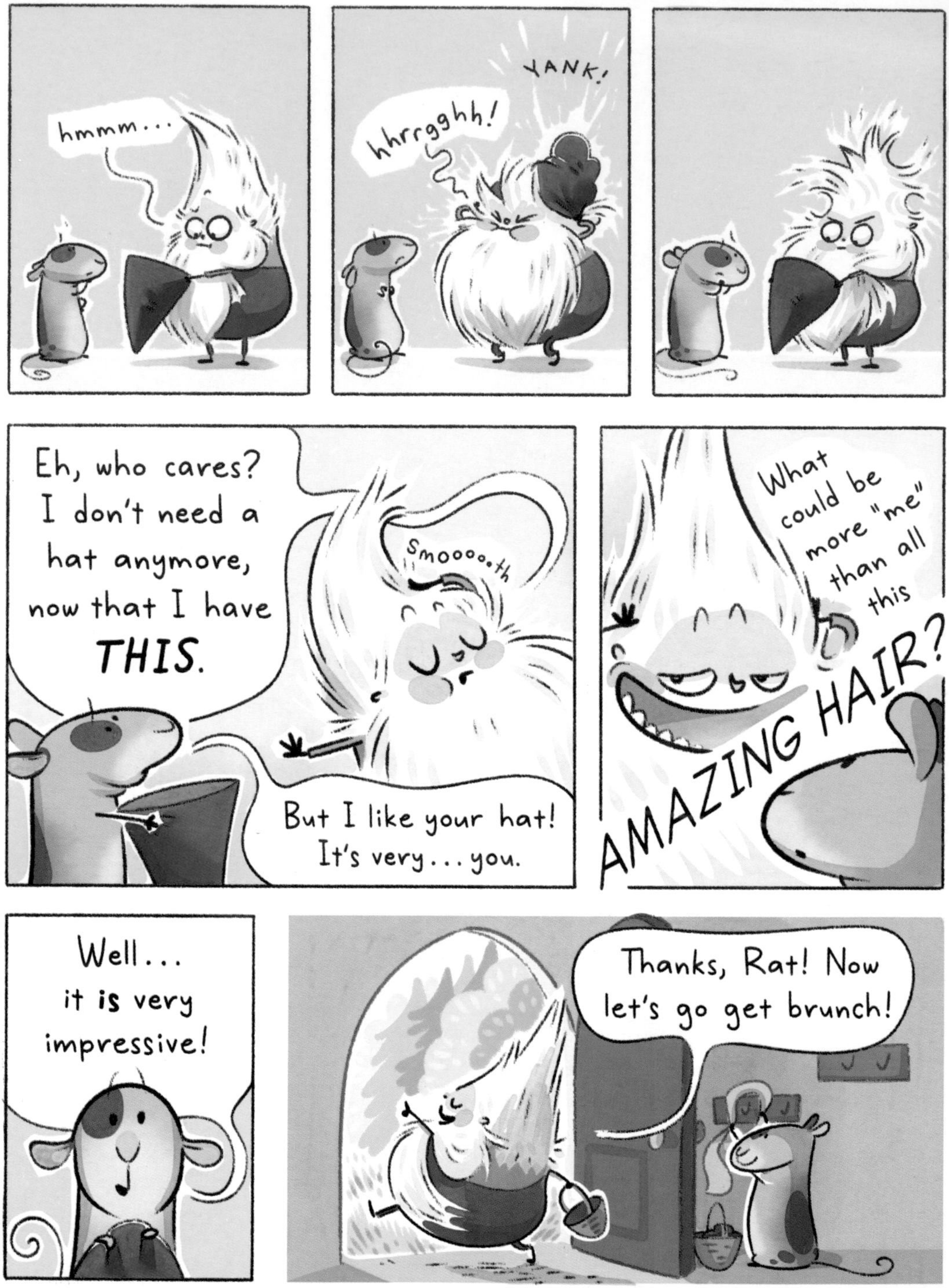

hmmm...
hhrrgghh!
YANK!
Eh, who cares? I don't need a hat anymore, now that I have THIS.
Smoooo...th
But I like your hat! It's very... you.
What could be more "me" than all this
AMAZING HAIR?
Well... it is very impressive!
Thanks, Rat! Now let's go get brunch!

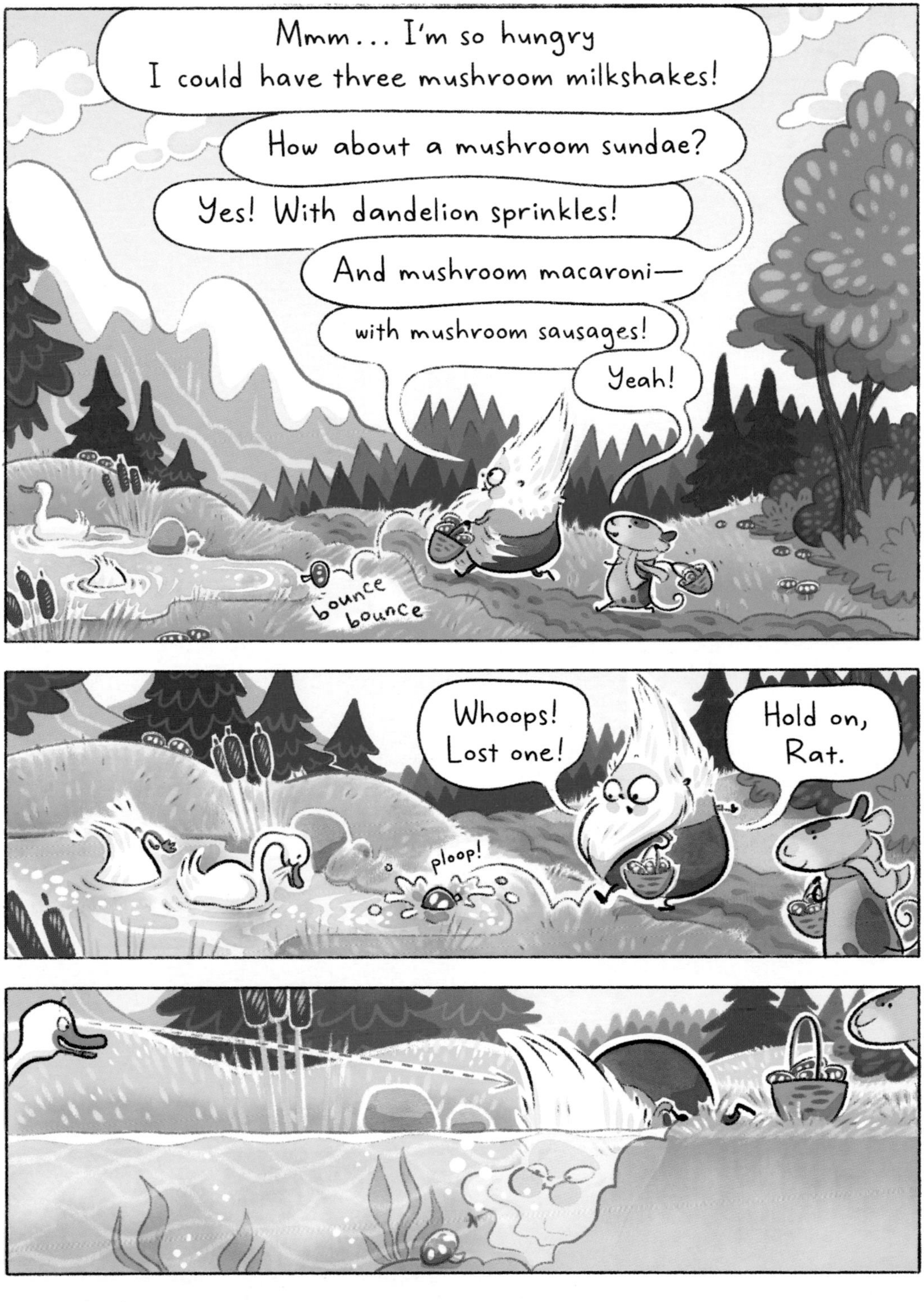
Mmm... I'm so hungry I could have three mushroom milkshakes!
How about a mushroom sundae?
Yes! With dandelion sprinkles!
And mushroom macaroni—
with mushroom sausages!
Yeah!
bounce bounce
Whoops! Lost one!
Hold on, Rat.
ploop!

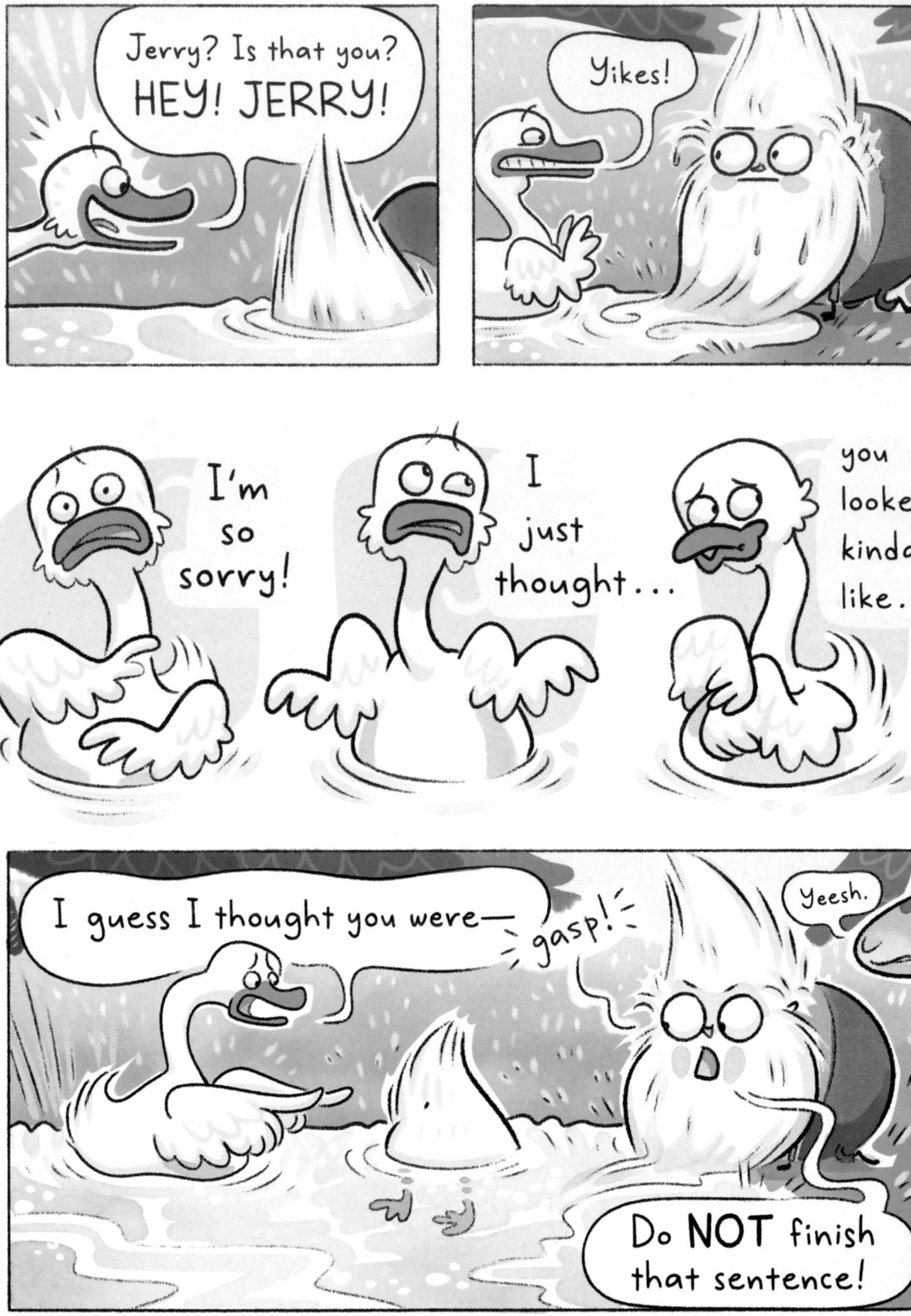
Jerry? Is that you? HEY! JERRY!
Yikes!
I'm so sorry!
I just thought...
you looked kinda like...
I guess I thought you were—
gasp!
Yeesh.
Do NOT finish that sentence!

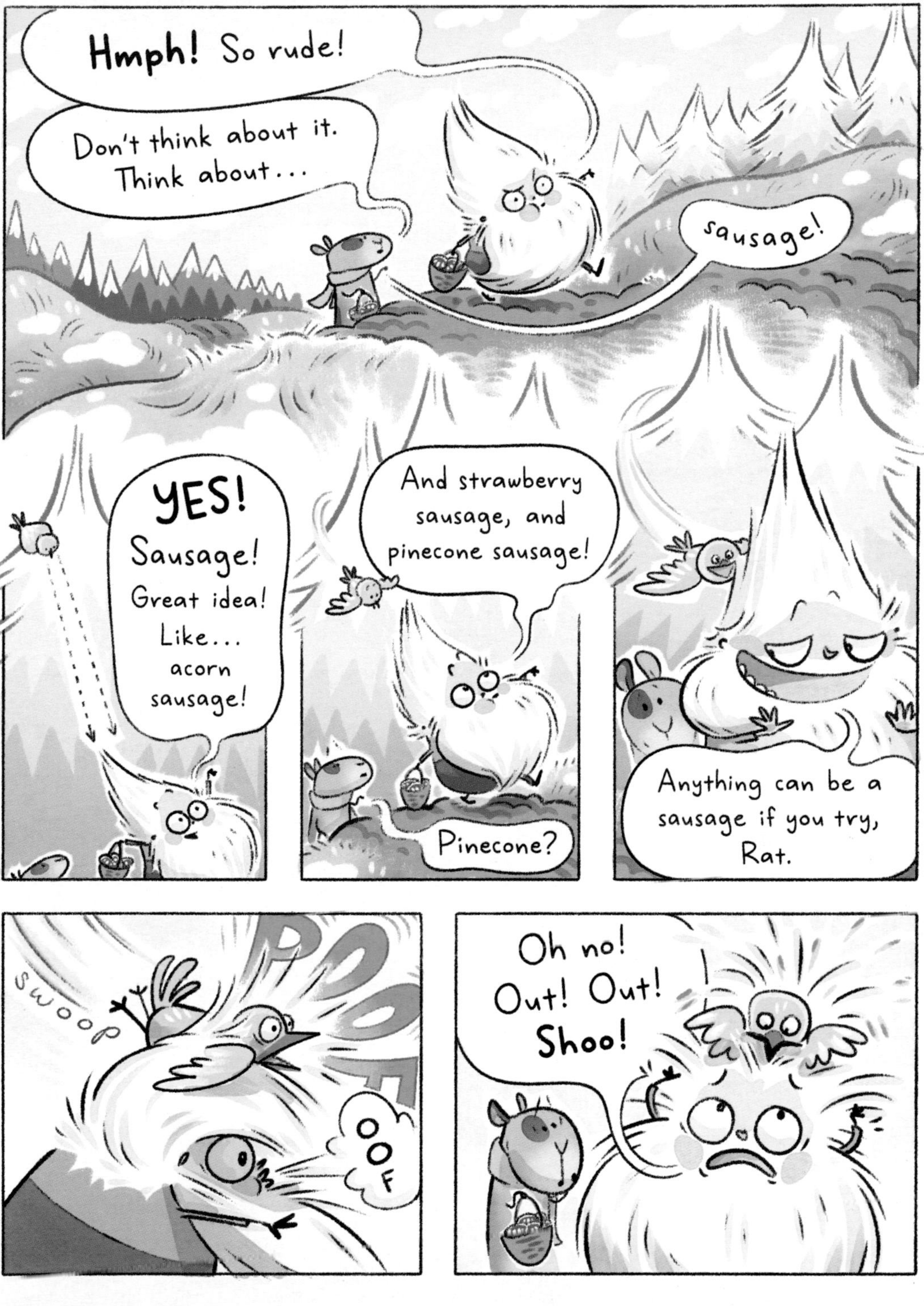
Hmph! So rude!
Don't think about it. Think about...
sausage!
YES! Sausage! Great idea! Like... acorn sausage!
And strawberry sausage, and pinecone sausage!
Pinecone?
Anything can be a sausage if you try, Rat.
swoop
POOF
OOF
Oh no! Out! Out! Shoo!

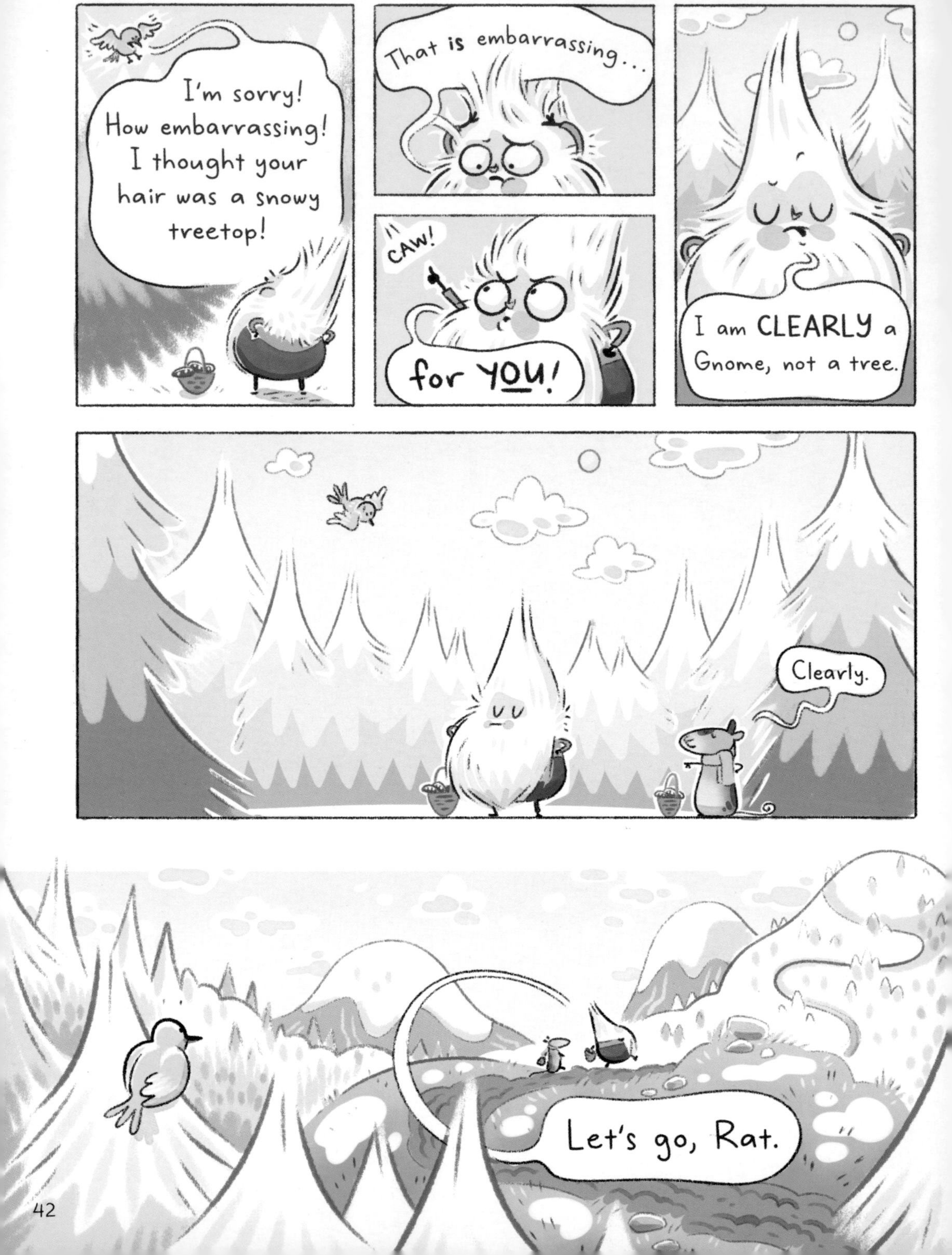
I'm sorry! How embarrassing! I thought your hair was a snowy treetop!
That is embarrassing...
CAW!
for YOU!
I am CLEARLY a Gnome, not a tree.
Clearly.
Let's go, Rat.

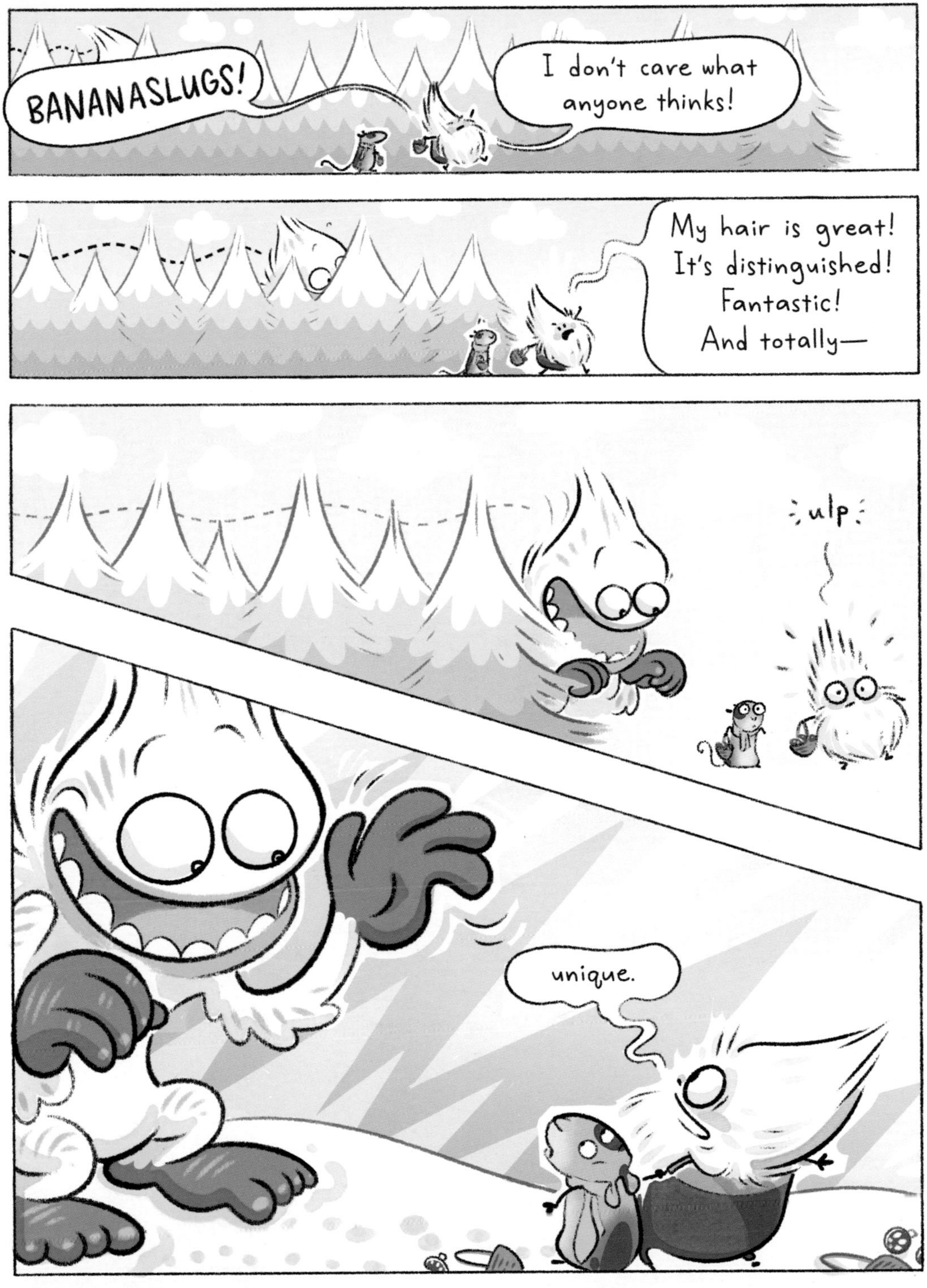
BANANASLUGS!
I don't care what anyone thinks!
My hair is great! It's distinguished! Fantastic! And totally—
ulp
unique.

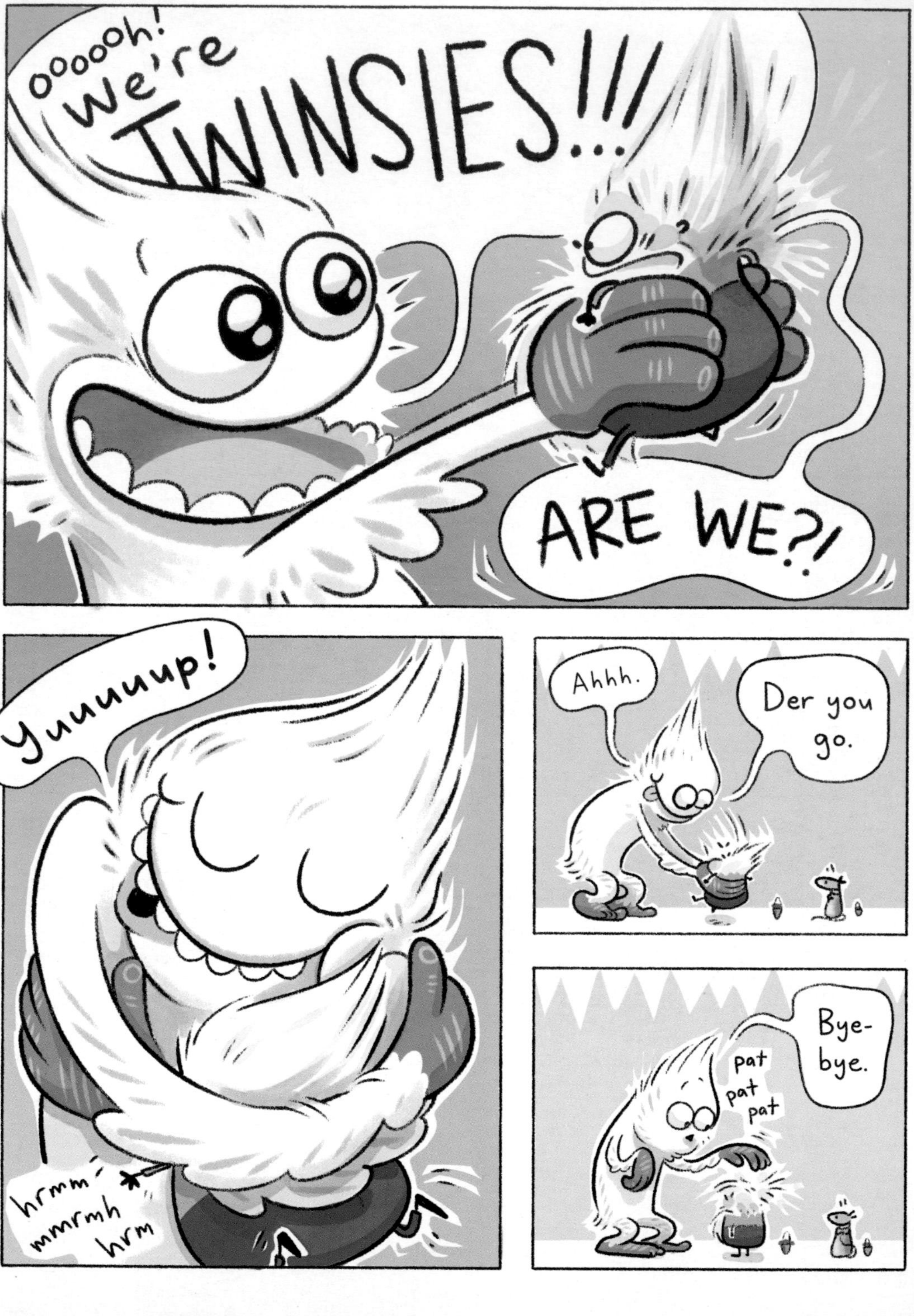

oooooh! We're TWINSIES!!!
ARE WE?!
Yuuuuup!
hrmm mmrmh hrm
Ahhh.
Der you go.
Bye-bye.
pat pat pat

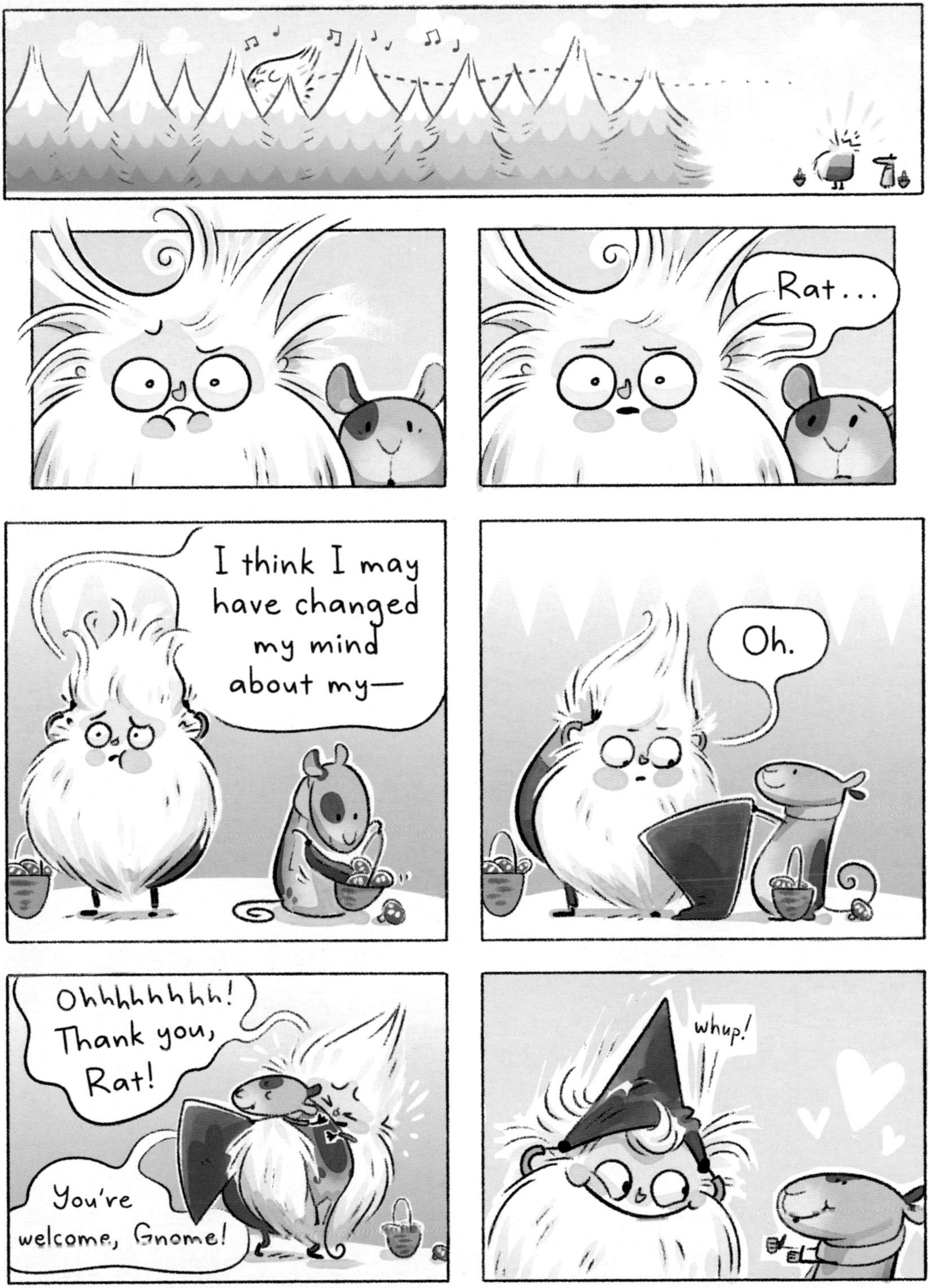
Rat...
I think I may have changed my mind about my—
Oh.
Ohhhhhhhh! Thank you, Rat!
You're welcome, Gnome!
whup!

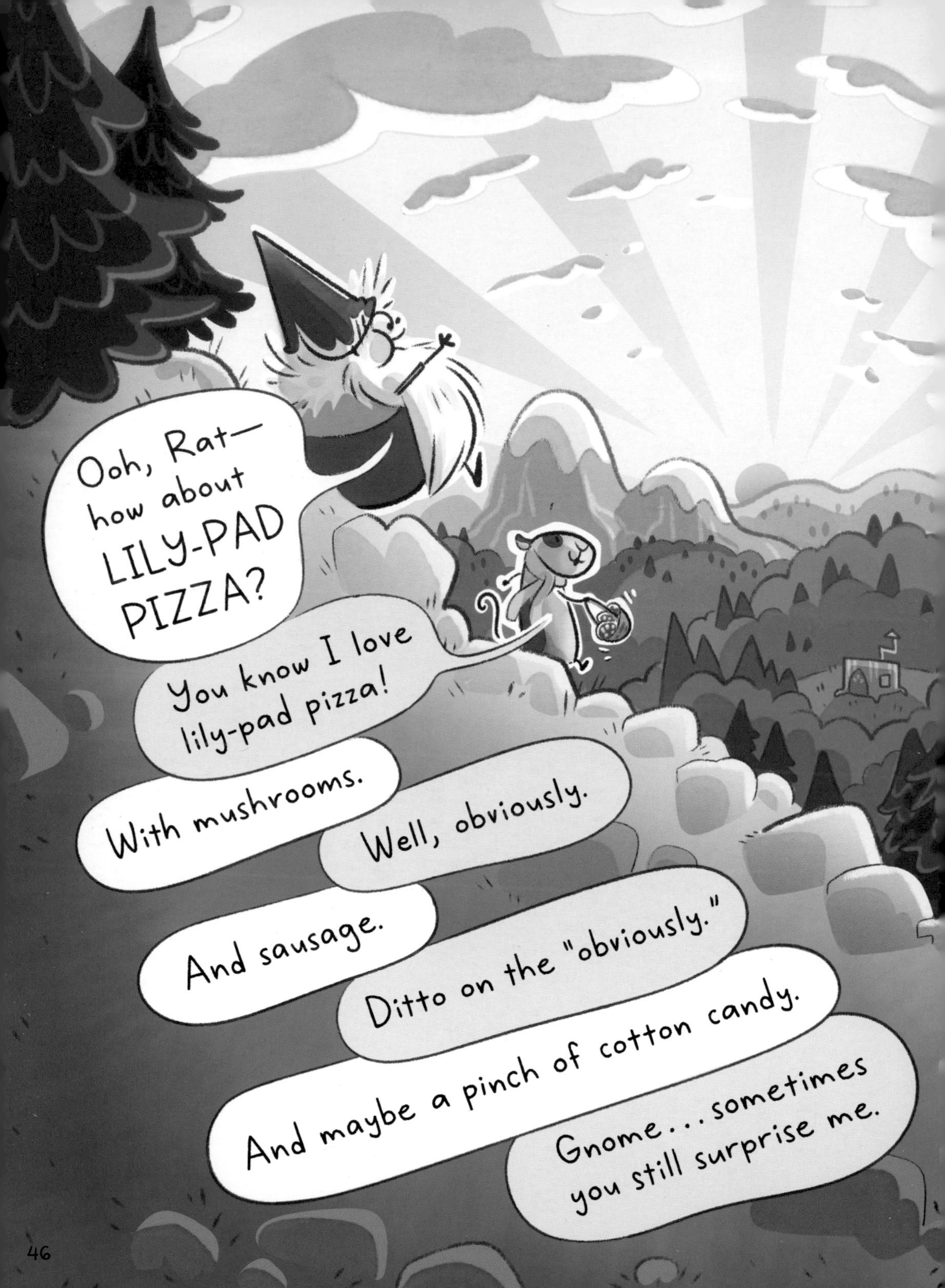
Ooh, Rat— how about LILY-PAD PIZZA?
You know I love lily-pad pizza!
With mushrooms.
Well, obviously.
And sausage.
Ditto on the "obviously."
And maybe a pinch of cotton candy.
Gnome... sometimes you still surprise me.

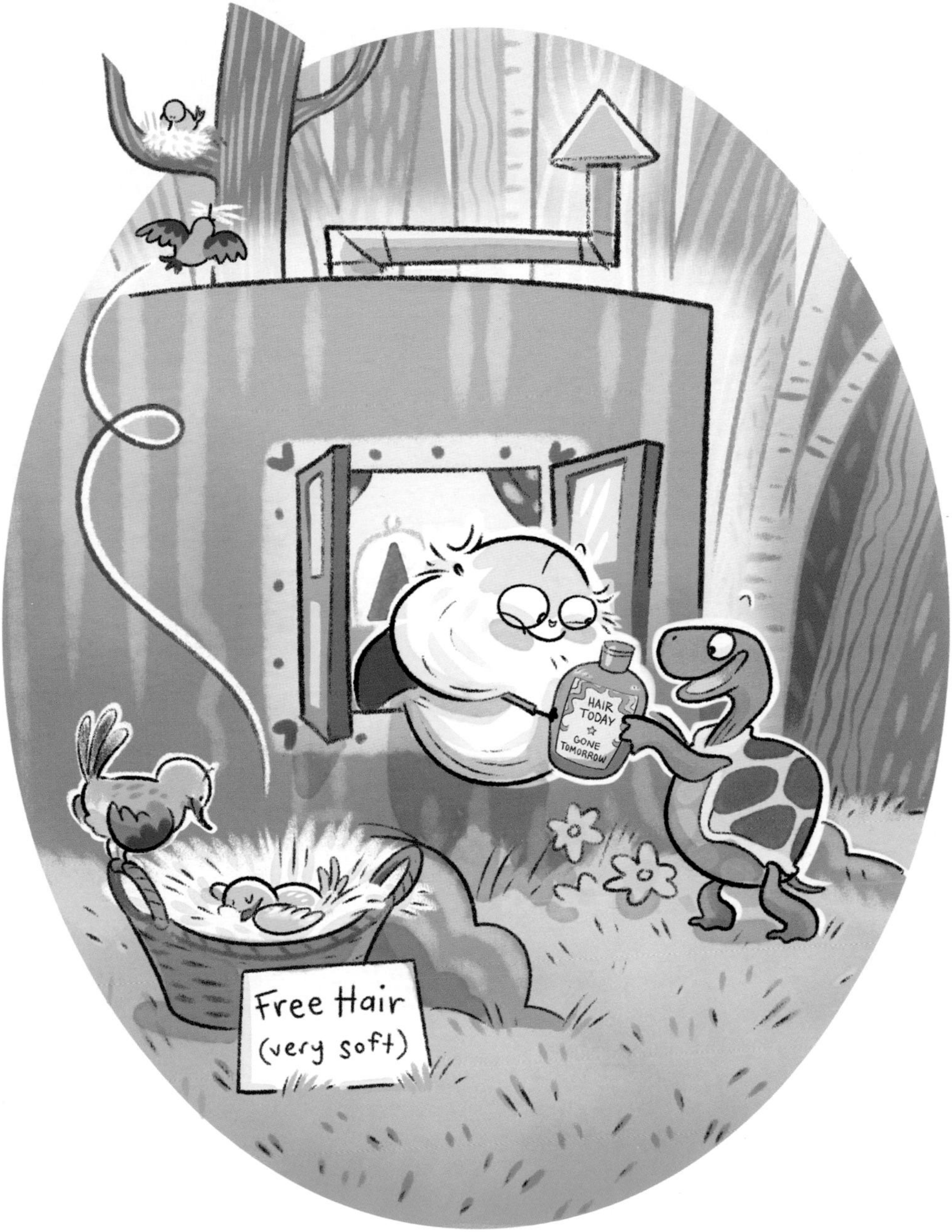
HAIR TODAY
GONE TOMORROW
Free Hair
(very soft)

CHAPTER 4

Gnome's New Hat

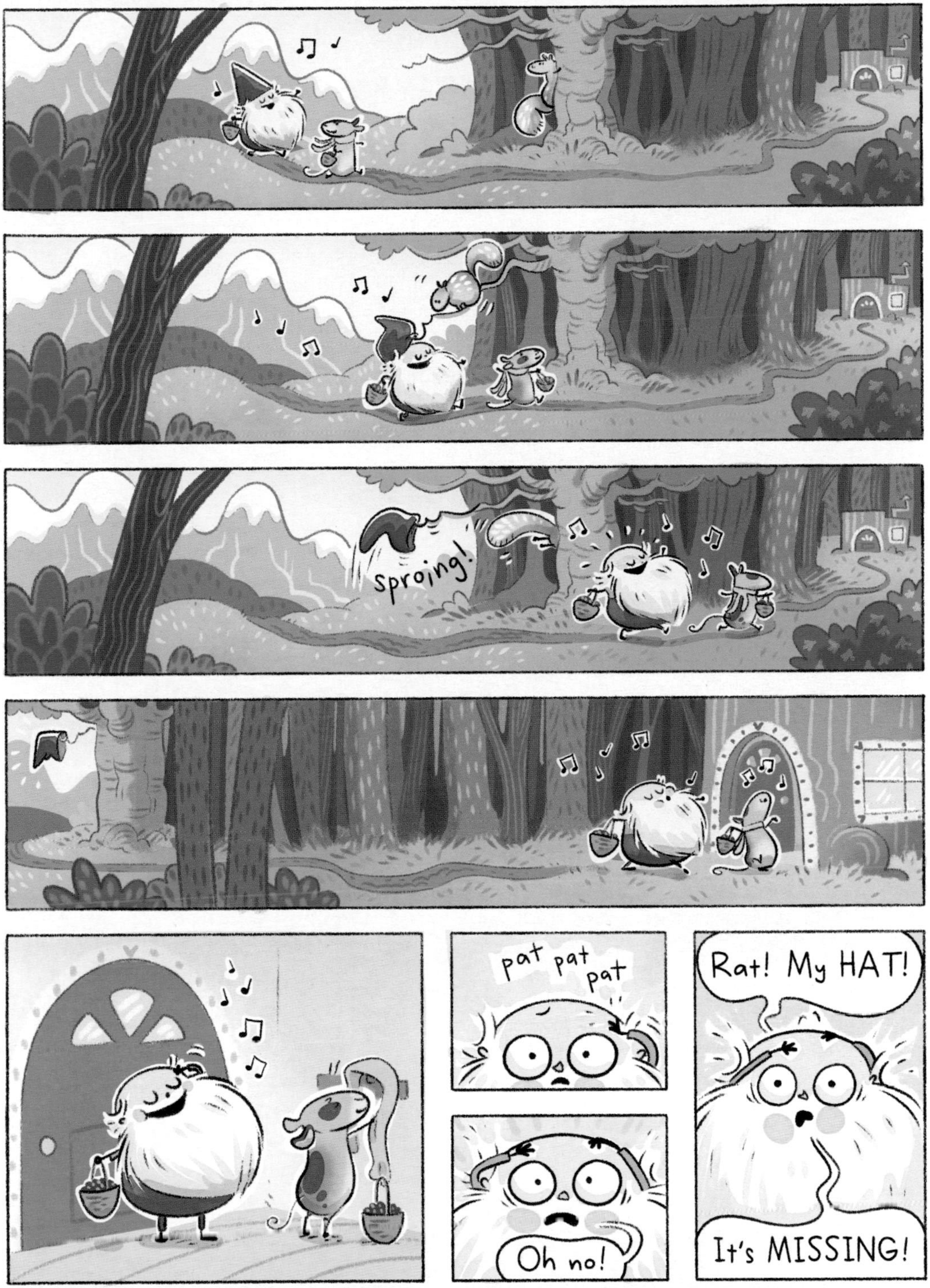
sproing!
pat pat pat
Oh no!
Rat! My HAT!
It's MISSING!

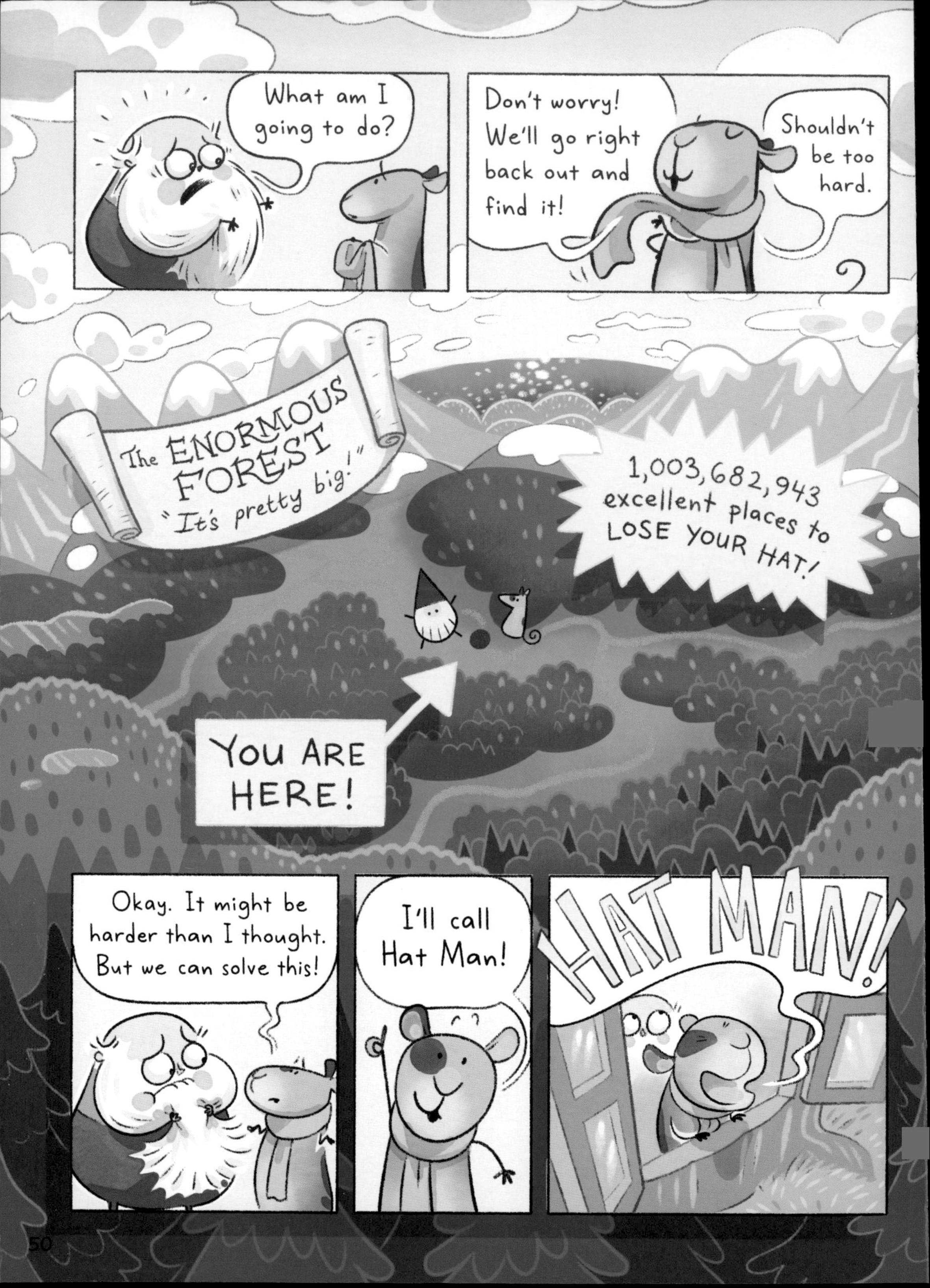
What am I going to do?
Don't worry! We'll go right back out and find it!
Shouldn't be too hard.
The ENORMOUS FOREST "It's pretty big!"
1,003,682,943 excellent places to LOSE YOUR HAT!
YOU ARE HERE!
Okay. It might be harder than I thought. But we can solve this!
I'll call Hat Man!
HAT MAN!

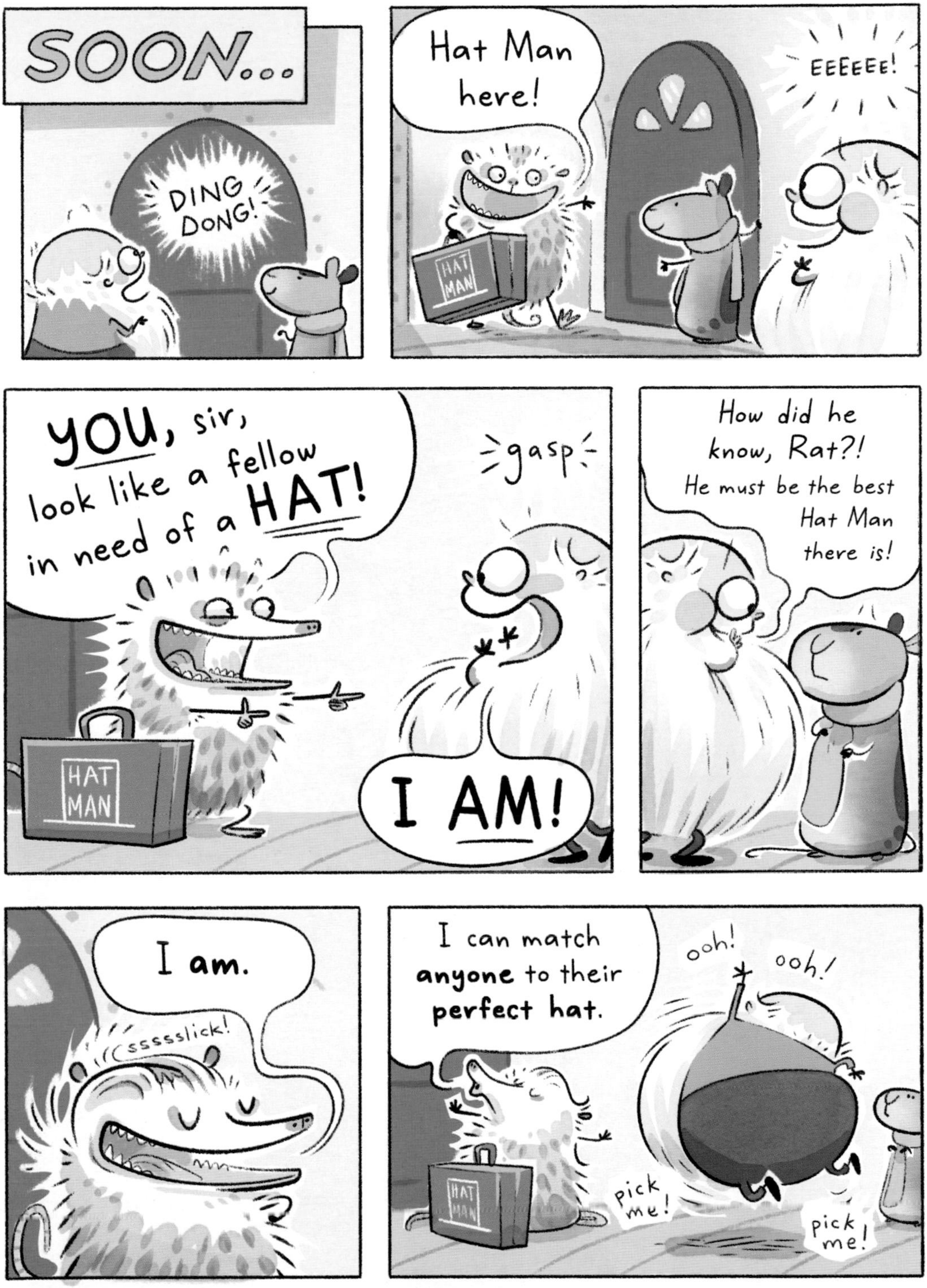
SOON...
DING DONG!
Hat Man here!
EEEEEE!
HAT MAN
YOU, sir, look like a fellow in need of a HAT!
gasp
I AM!
HAT MAN
How did he know, Rat?! He must be the best Hat Man there is!
I am.
ssssslick!
I can match anyone to their perfect hat.
ooh!
ooh!
HAT MAN
pick me!
pick me!

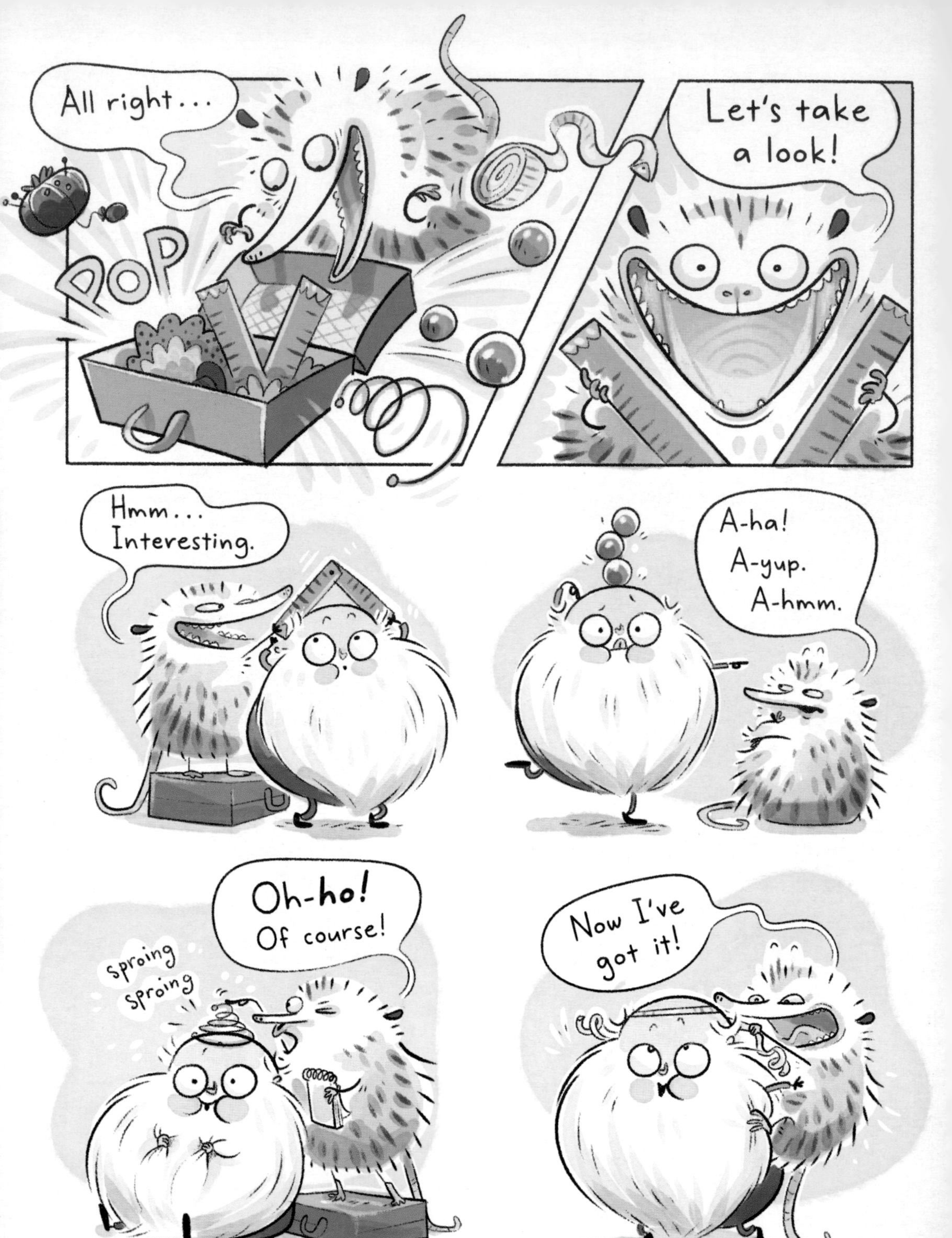
All right...
POP
Let's take a look!
Hmm... Interesting.
A-ha! A-yup. A-hmm.
Oh-**ho**! Of course!
sproing sproing
Now I've got it!

Well!

You are one lucky Gnome!

I AM?

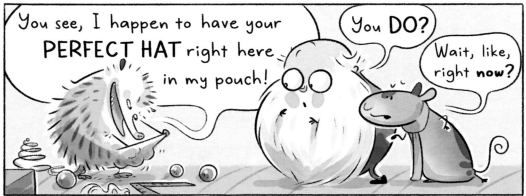

You see, I happen to have your **PERFECT HAT** right here in my pouch!

You DO?

Wait, like, right **now**?

YES! Beneath this sheet is your **PERFECT HAT MATCH!**

gassssssp!

Just saying, that seems like a **really** big coincidence.

Wanna see?

yes yes yes yes yes yes y yes yes yes yes yes ye yes yes yes

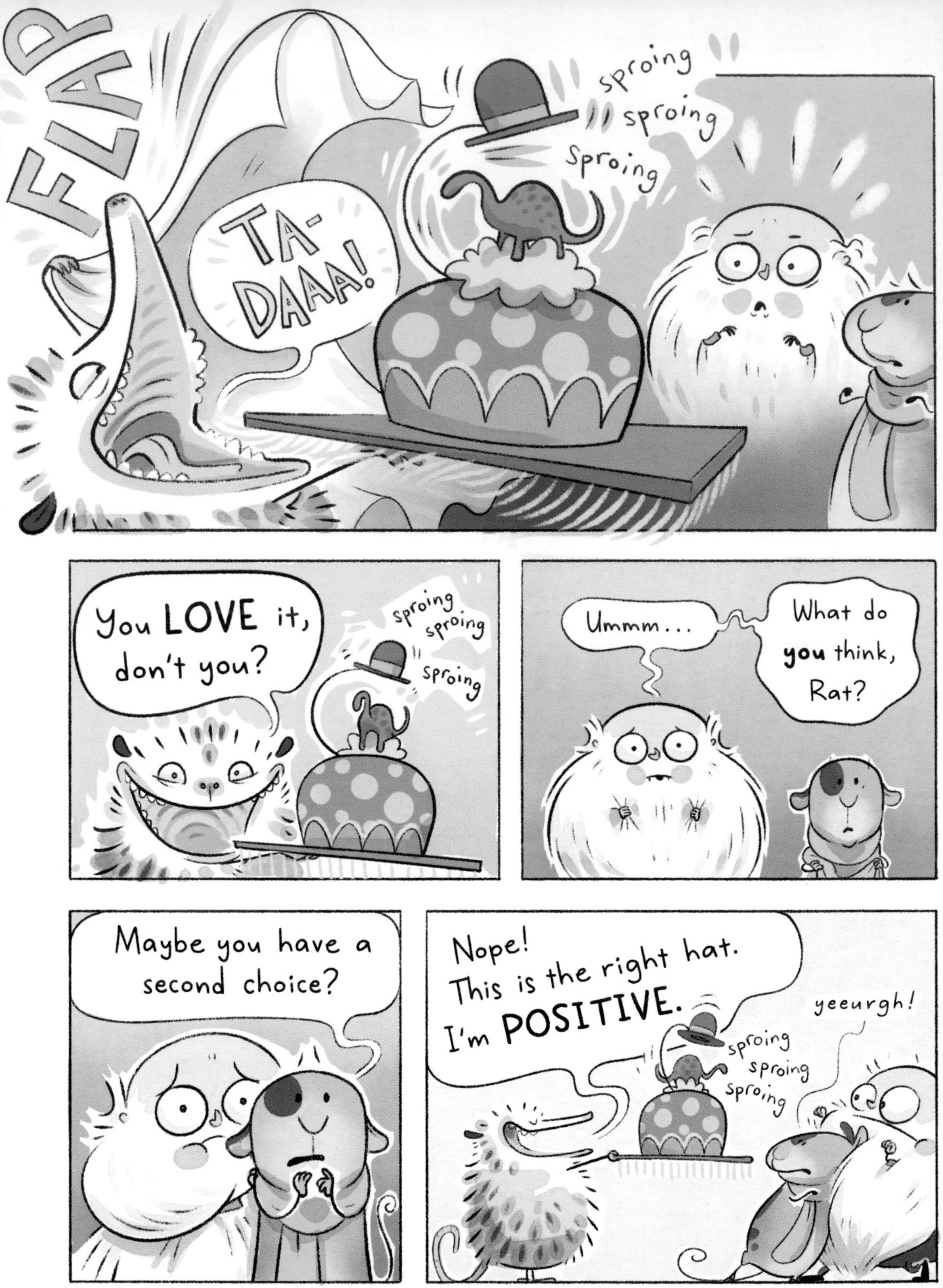
FLAP
TA-DAAA!
sproing
sproing
sproing
You LOVE it, don't you?
sproing
sproing
sproing
Ummm...
What do you think, Rat?
Maybe you have a second choice?
Nope! This is the right hat. I'm POSITIVE.
sproing
sproing
sproing
yeeurgh!

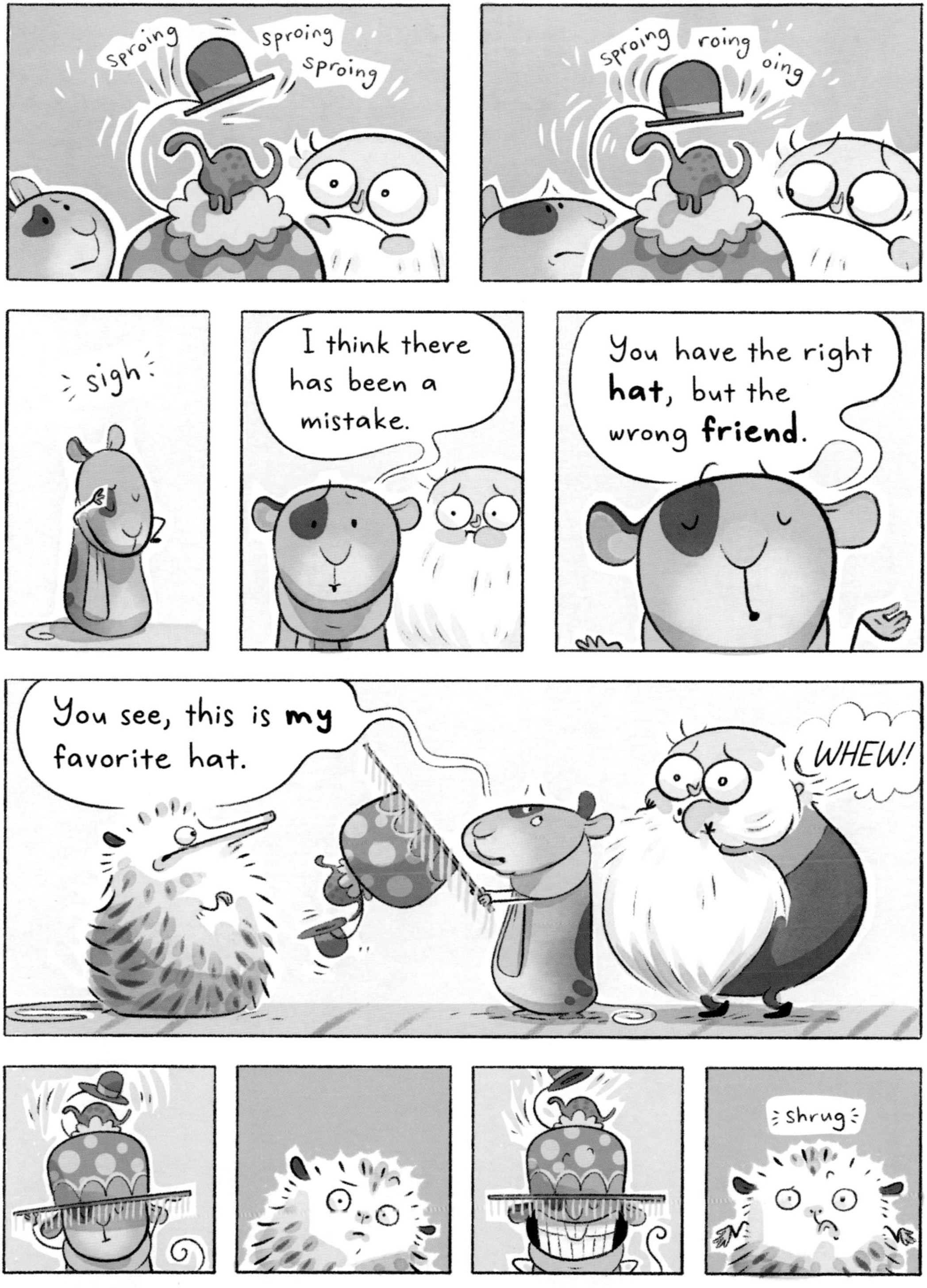
sproing
sproing
sproing
sproing
roing
oing
sigh
I think there has been a mistake.
You have the right **hat**, but the wrong **friend**.
You see, this is **my** favorite hat.
WHEW!
shrug

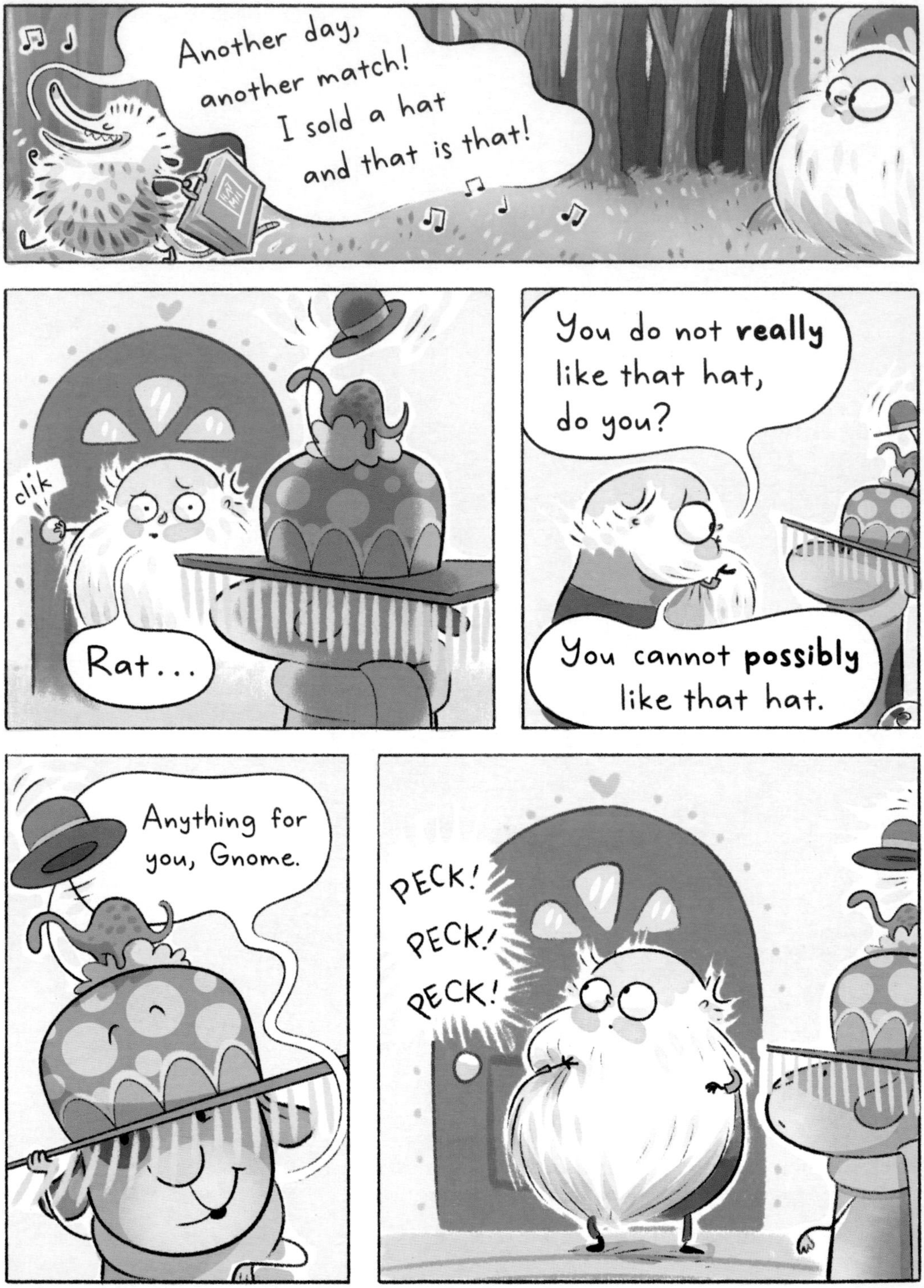
Another day, another match! I sold a hat and that is that!
clik
Rat...
You do not **really** like that hat, do you?
You cannot **possibly** like that hat.
Anything for you, Gnome.
PECK!
PECK!
PECK!

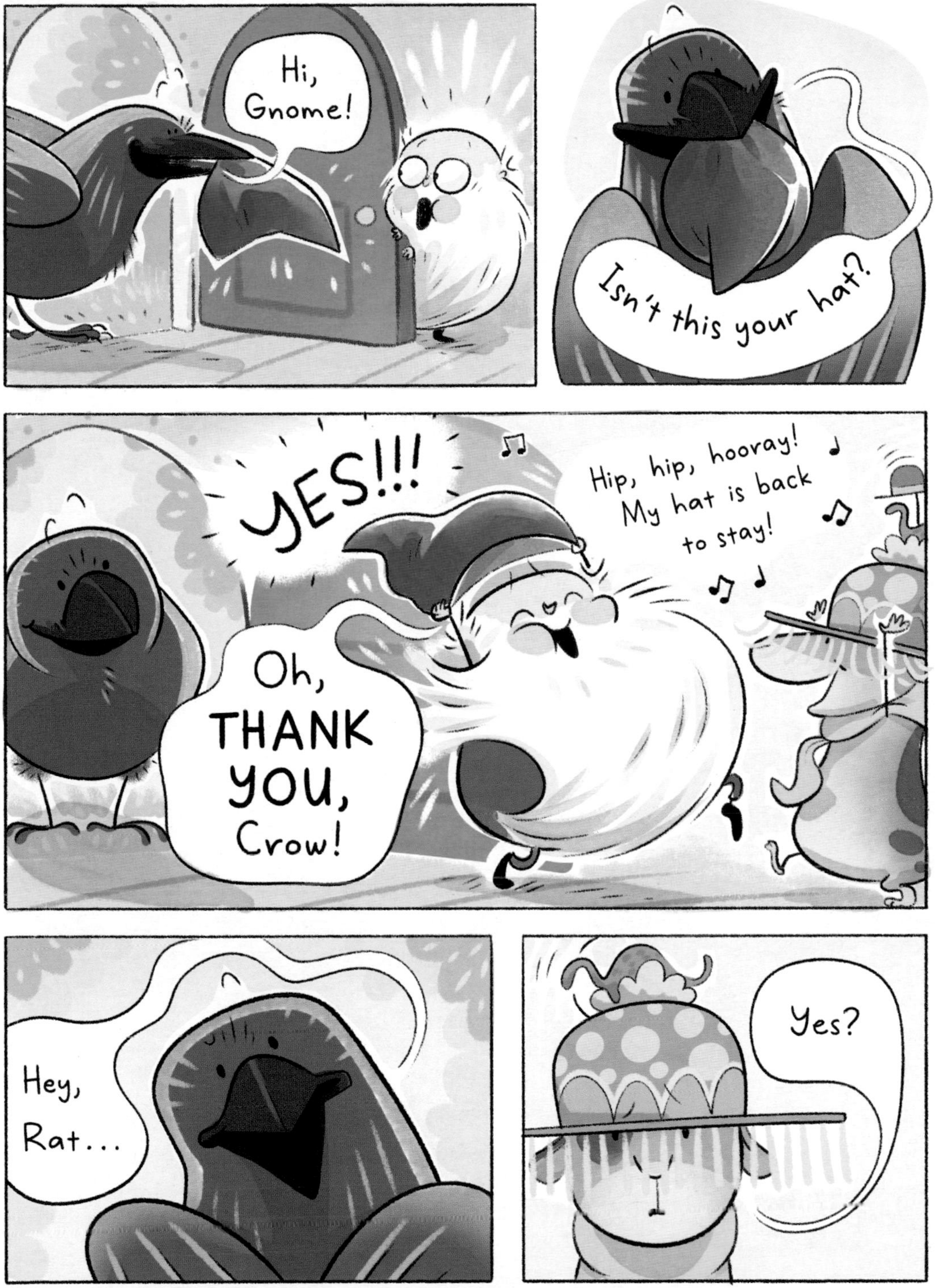
Hi, Gnome!
Isn't this your hat?
YES!!!
Hip, hip, hooray! My hat is back to stay!
Oh, THANK YOU, Crow!
Hey, Rat...
Yes?

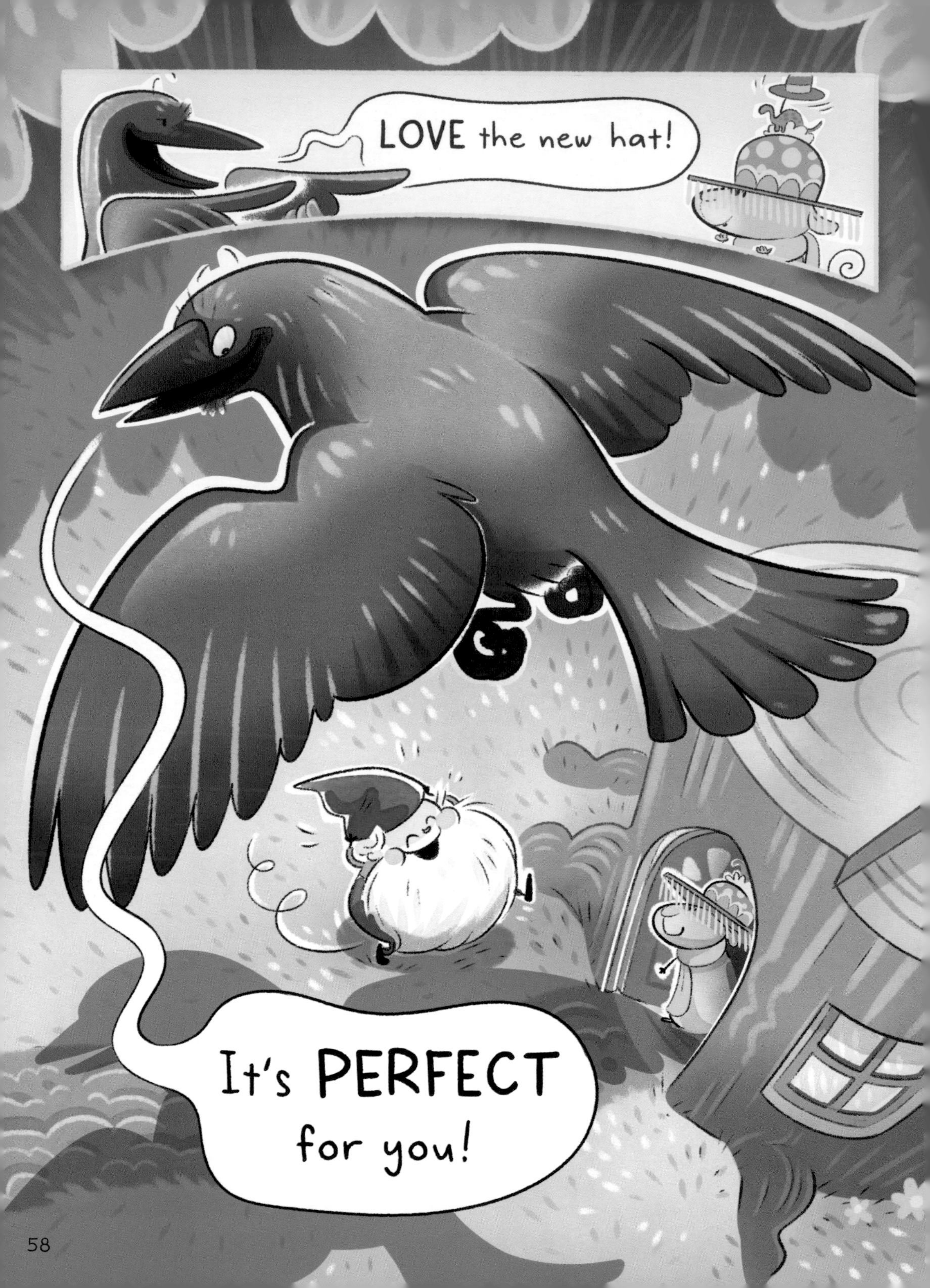
LOVE the new hat!
It's PERFECT for you!

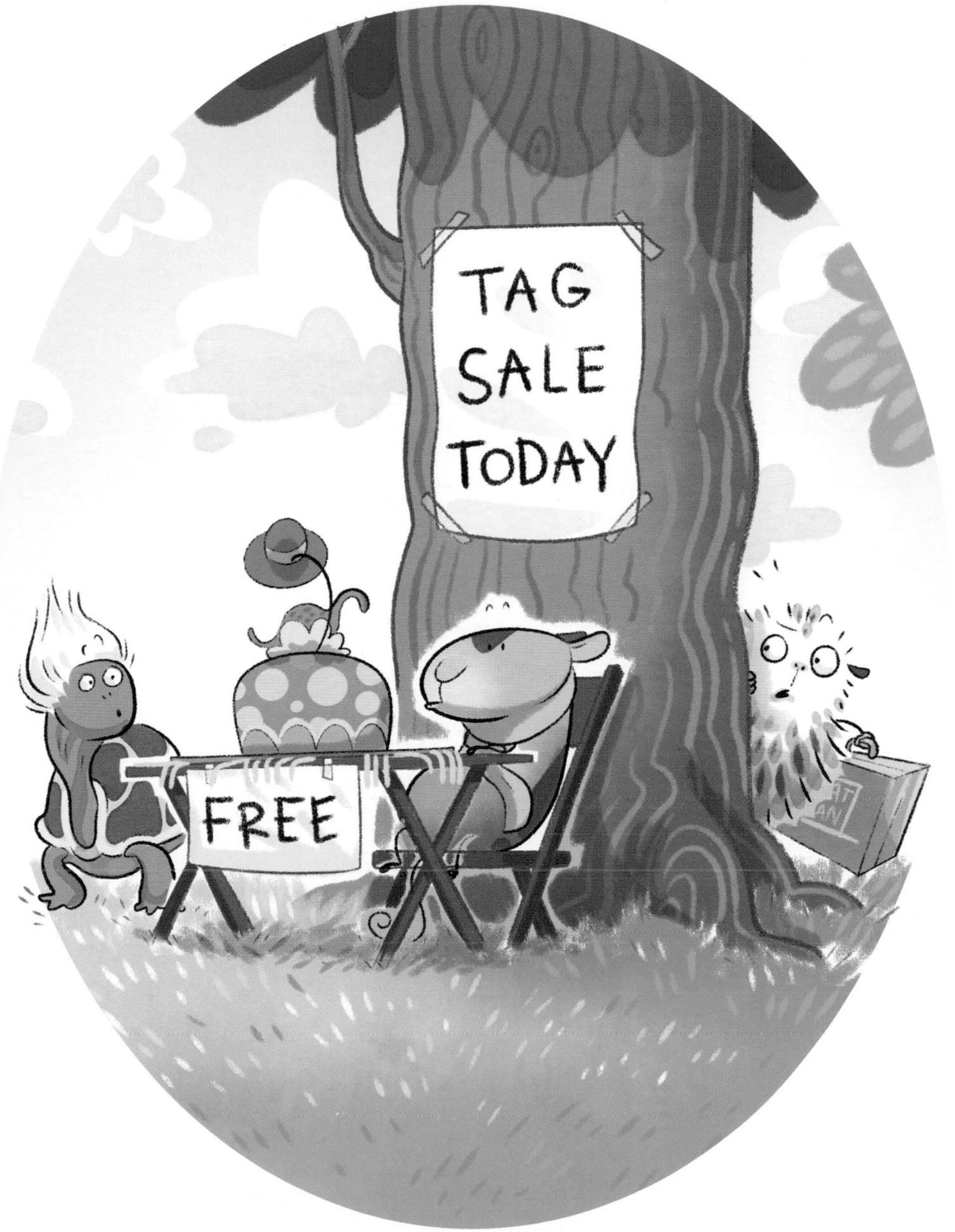
TAG
SALE
TODAY
FREE

CHAPTER 5

Back Hat It Again

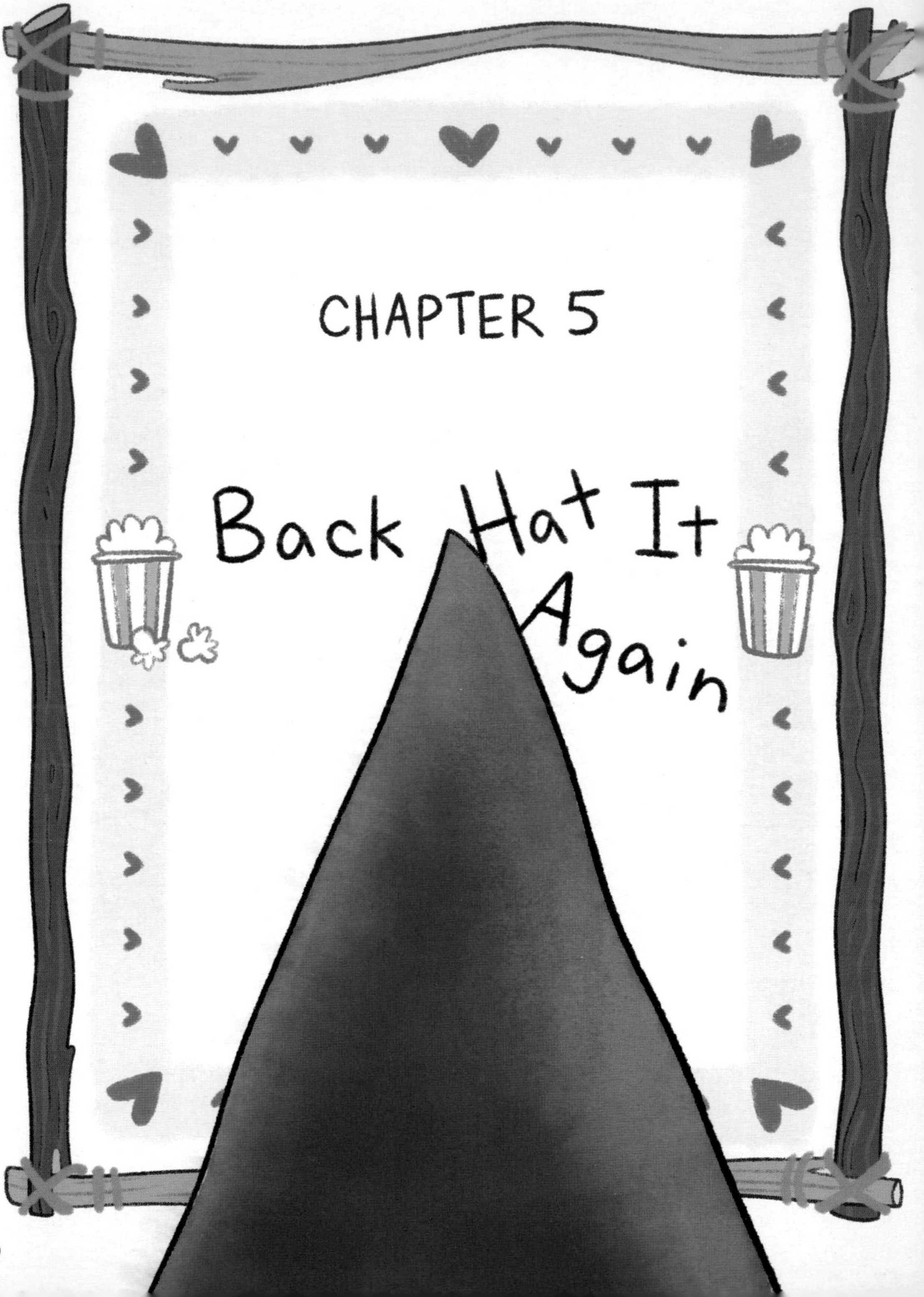

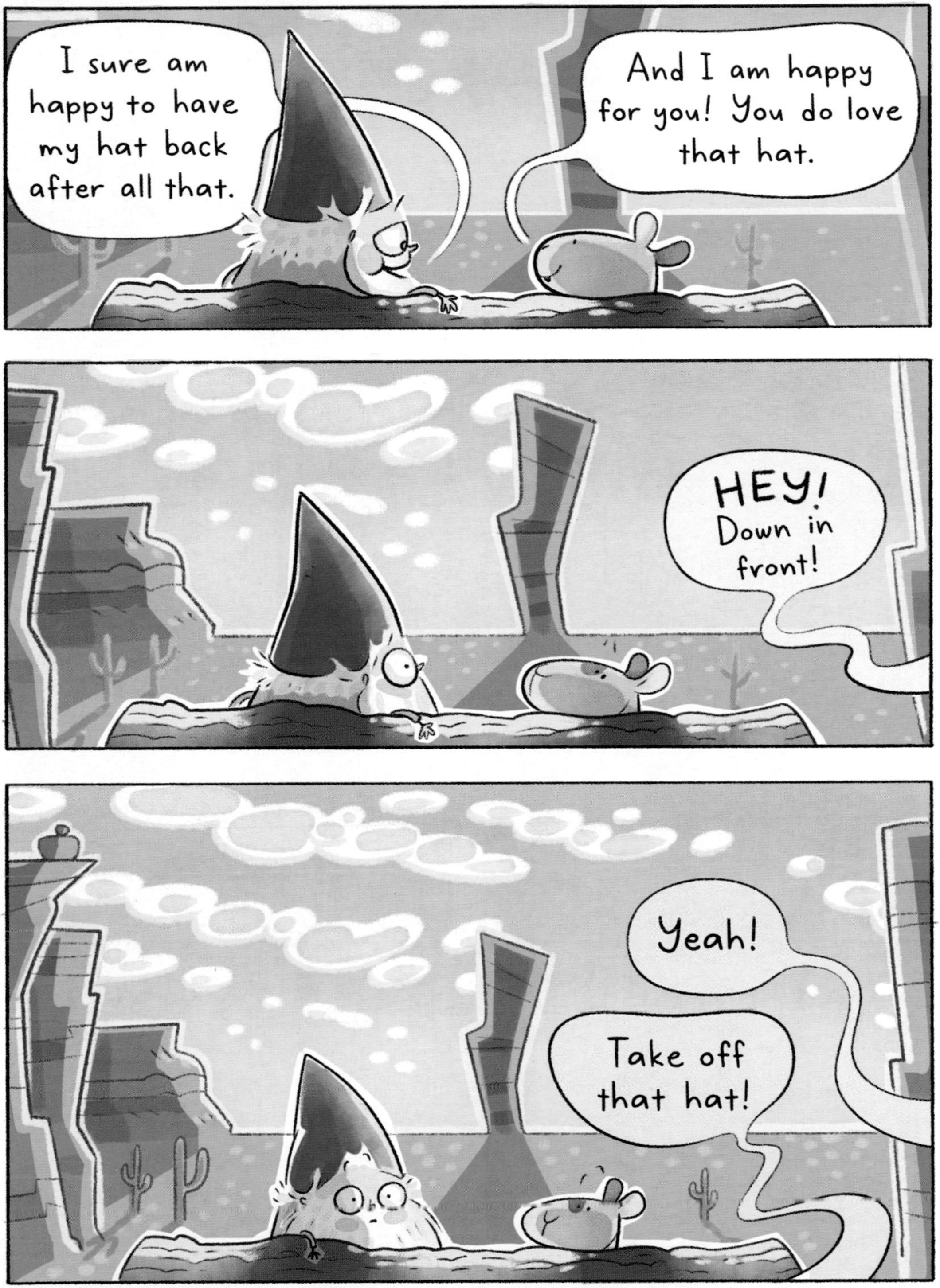

I sure am happy to have my hat back after all that.
And I am happy for you! You do love that hat.
HEY! Down in front!
Yeah!
Take off that hat!

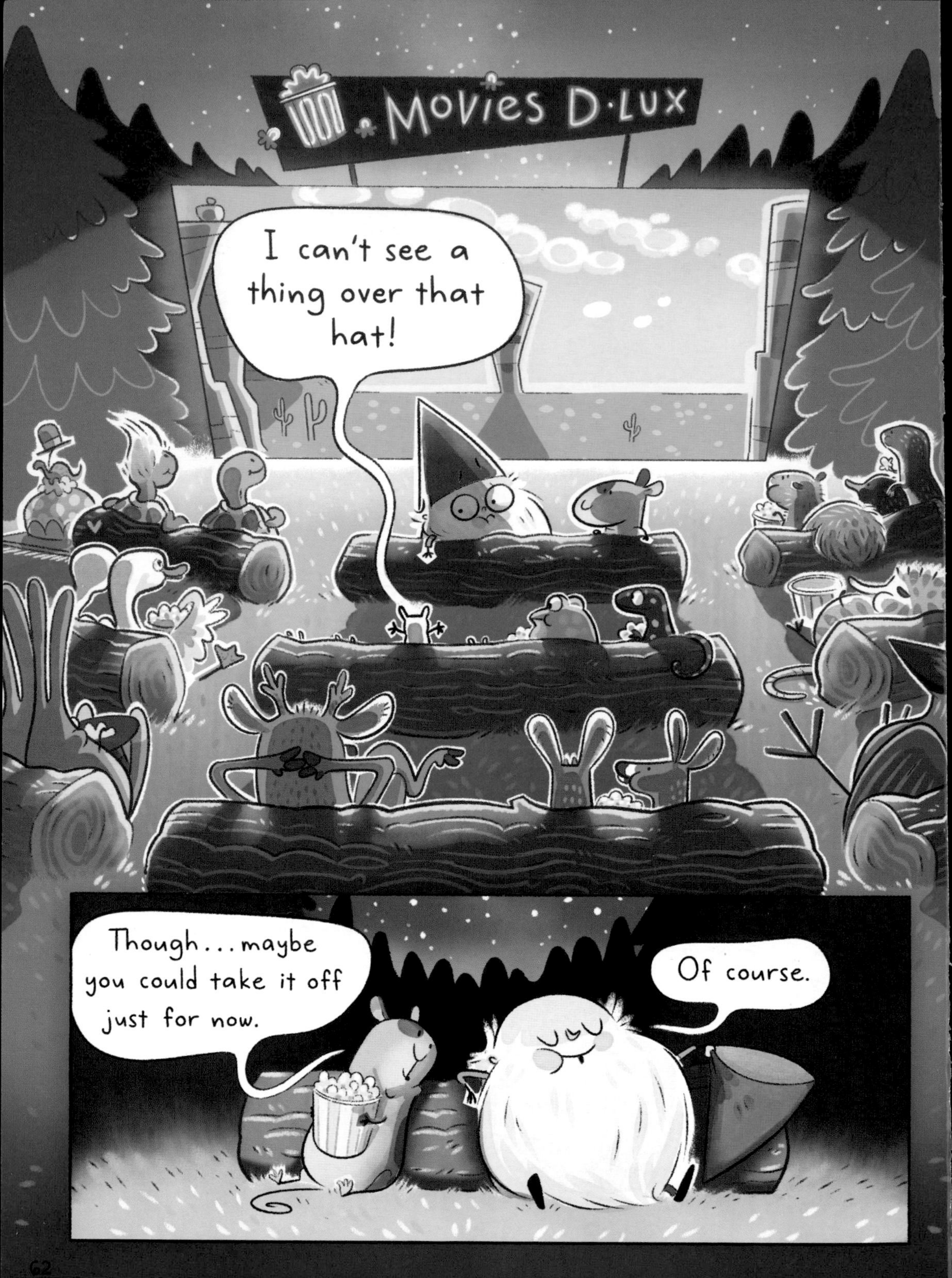
MOVIES D·LUX
I can't see a thing over that hat!
Though... maybe you could take it off just for now.
Of course.

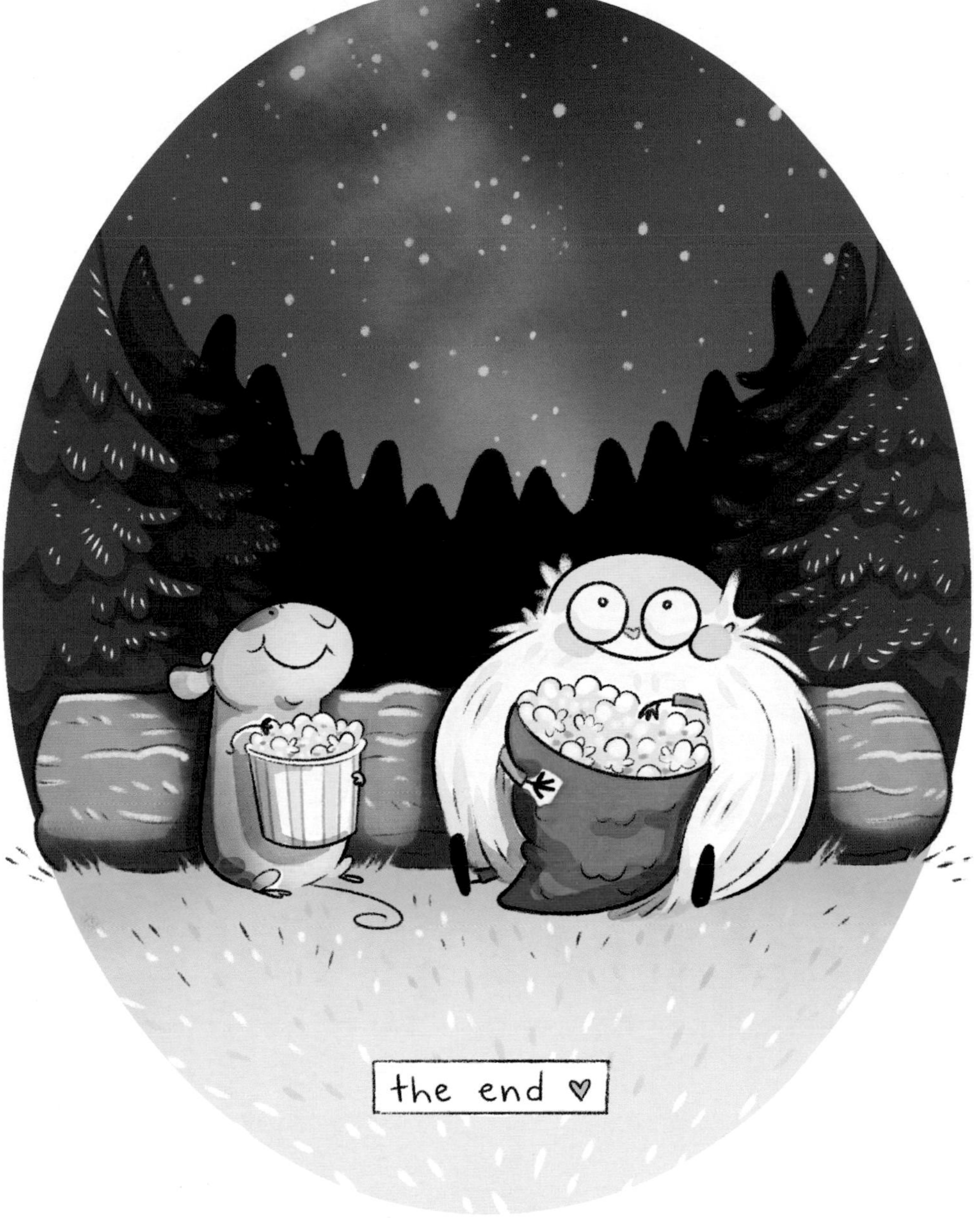
the end ♡

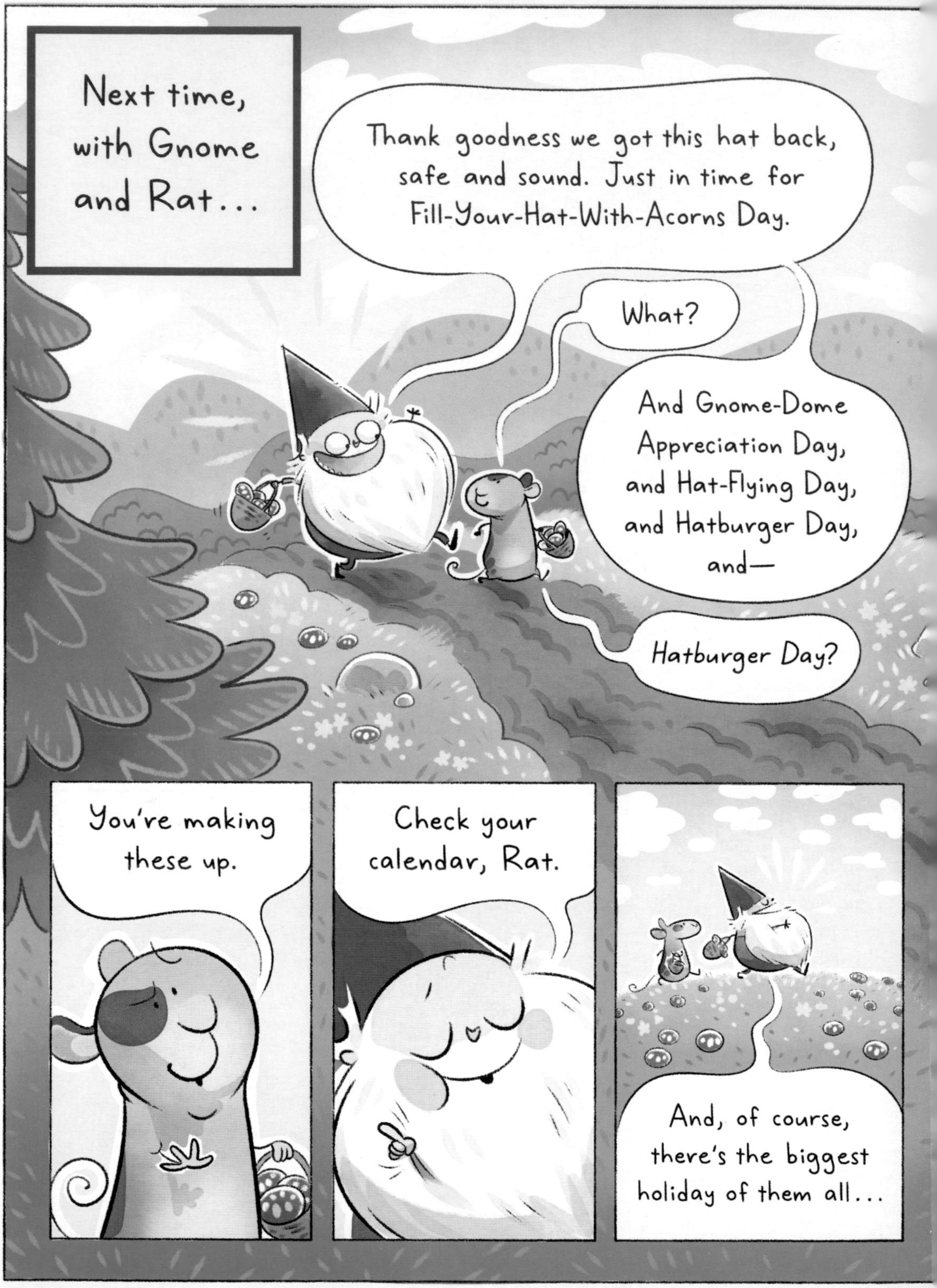
Next time, with Gnome and Rat...
Thank goodness we got this hat back, safe and sound. Just in time for Fill-Your-Hat-With-Acorns Day.
What?
And Gnome-Dome Appreciation Day, and Hat-Flying Day, and Hatburger Day, and—
Hatburger Day?
You're making these up.
Check your calendar, Rat.
And, of course, there's the biggest holiday of them all...

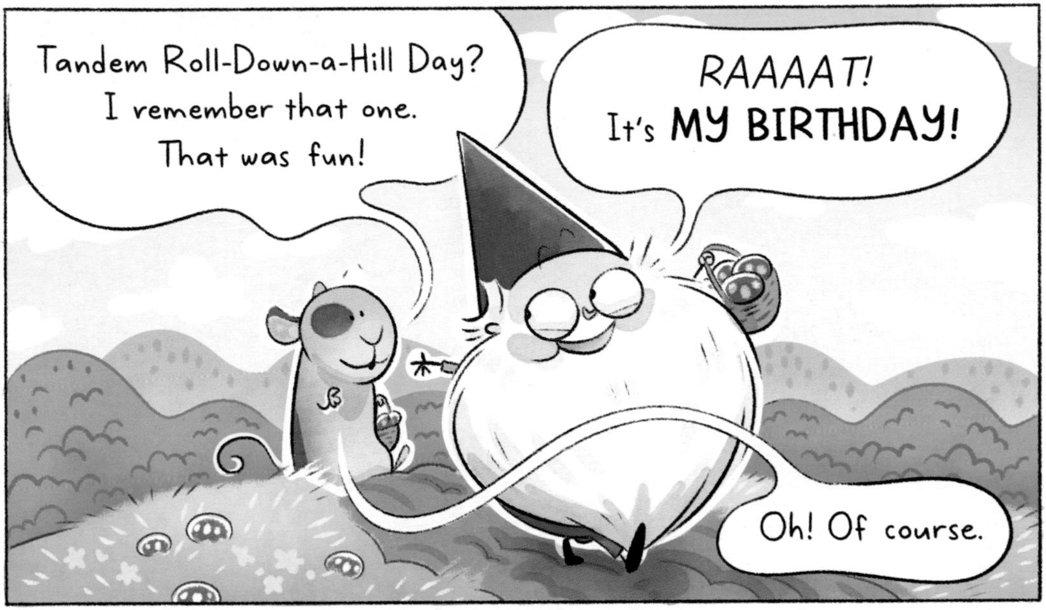
Tandem Roll-Down-a-Hill Day? I remember that one. That was fun!
RAAAAT! It's MY BIRTHDAY!
Oh! Of course.

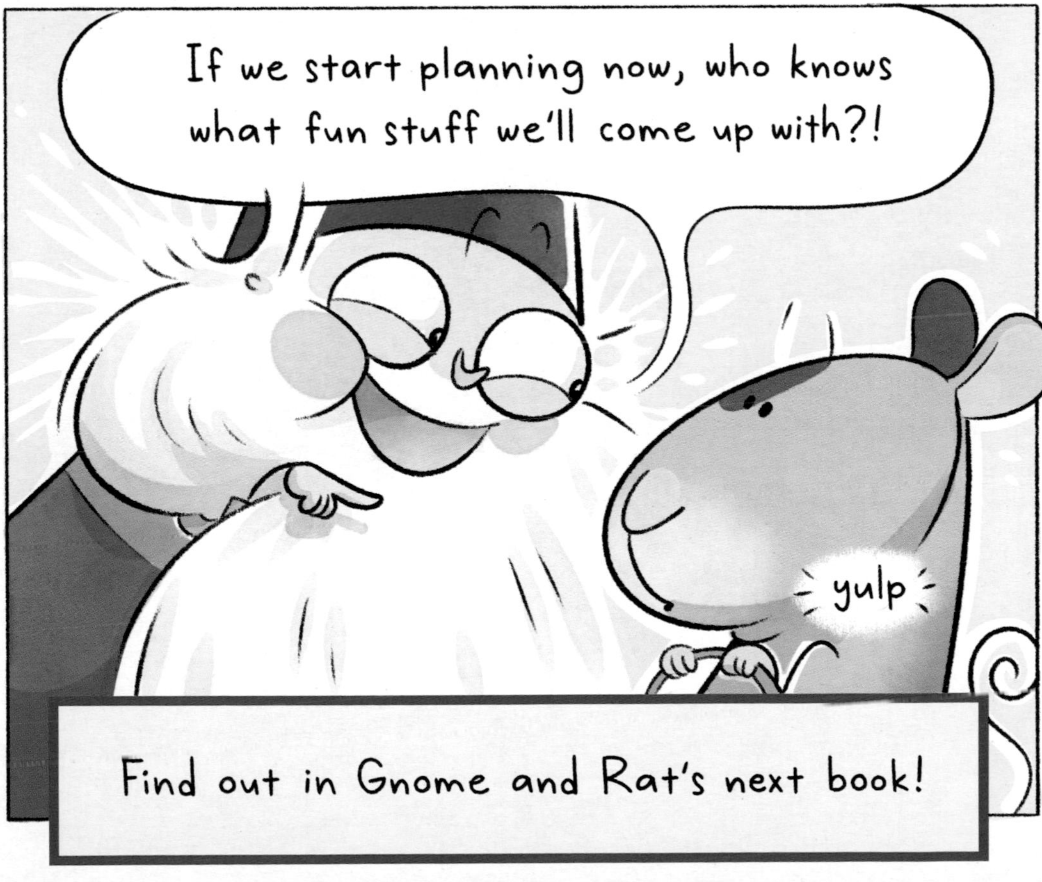
If we start planning now, who knows what fun stuff we'll come up with?!
yulp
Find out in Gnome and Rat's next book!

How to Braid Your Beard

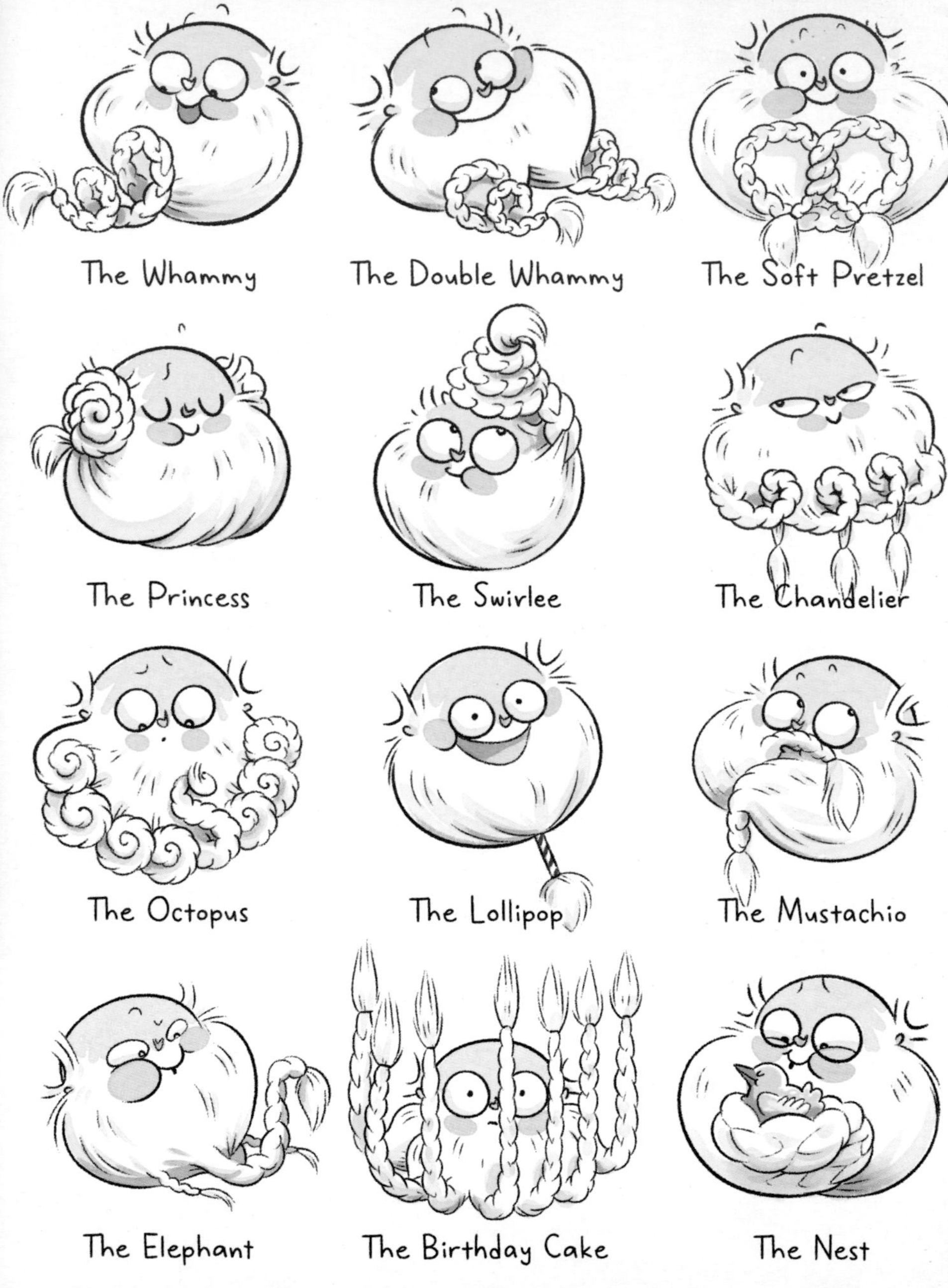
The Whammy
The Double Whammy
The Soft Pretzel
The Princess
The Swirlee
The Chandelier
The Octopus
The Lollipop
The Mustachio
The Elephant
The Birthday Cake
The Nest